THE CASE OF THE

CAGED COCKERS

A Thousand Islands Doggy Inn Mystery

B.R. SNOW

ISBN: 978-1-942691-08-2
Website:www.brsnow.net/
Twitter: @BernSnow
Facebook: facebook.com/bernsnow

Cover Design: Reggie Cullen
Cover Photo: James R. Miller

Other Books by B.R. Snow

The Thousand Islands Doggy Inn Mysteries

- The Case of the Abandoned Aussie
- The Case of the Brokenhearted Bulldog

The Damaged Po$$e Series

- American Midnight
- Larrikin Gene
- Sneaker World
- Summerman
- The Duplicates

Other books

- Divorce Hotel
- Either Ore

To Reggie

Chapter 1

On a frigid, snowy Thursday, Thanksgiving came and went. The entire day was filled with great conversation in the company of good friends in a warm house and a menu that even the all-too-modest Chef Claire had to admit was one of her best. Friday's dinner was a repeat of the previous day's turkey with all the fixings that was as good if not better than the original. Between the two dinners, Josie and I embarked on a wild flurry of snacking that shattered all of our previous records for gluttony and bad table manners that caused my mother, at one point on Friday afternoon, to wonder out loud who the alien was that bore a striking resemblance to the daughter she had raised.

We had dressed for Thanksgiving dinner, but by the time the pumpkin trifle and an apple pie topped with a brandy caramel sauce that was a total knee-buckler were served, Josie and I had swapped out our dinner attire for the snacker pants we were still wearing when the weekend rolled around.

The pants were taking quite a beating this year but seemed to be holding up.

Friday started with a breakfast turkey quiche that disappeared in ten minutes. That was followed later in the day by a turkey sandwich, a bowl of pumpkin trifle, a hot turkey sandwich with gravy, a slice of apple pie, then another sandwich in that order followed by a long nap.

Or as my mother called it; a tryptophan coma.

I had to hand it to her. She was definitely on her game this holiday season.

Friday night, Chef Claire made a turkey gumbo that brought tears to my eyes.

Saturday, she made two different kinds of turkey soup. One was a traditional version; the other was a rustic Italian tomato bread soup with homemade turkey sausage. Josie and I were still debating which one was better, but since there was still half a pot left of each, we weren't in any hurry to make a final decision.

On Sunday night, I hit the wall and was officially turkeyed out. Josie had agreed, but I think she lied to me because the next morning I'd caught her in her office at the Inn gnawing on a turkey leg.

Now I was sitting at the dinner table across from Josie and wondering aloud how was it possible for me to be hungry. Chef Claire came in from the kitchen carrying a tray filled with bite-sized appetizers that were steaming hot. She set them down on the table, and I stared down at the tray, then looked up at Chef Claire.

"I've wanted to test this idea out for a long time," Chef Claire said.

"Well, if you're looking for two guinea pigs to try it out on, you've come to the right place," Josie said.

"What are they?" I said, staring lovingly at the fresh baked objects that were no more than two inches long.

"Try one, and then you tell me," Chef Claire said.

Needing no encouragement, I picked one up and popped it into my mouth. As I chewed, a flood of memories raced through my head.

"That's incredible," I said. "How did you do that?"

Chef Claire beamed with pride and selected one from the tray. Josie followed suit. As she chewed, she stared at Chef Claire.

"I call them One Bite Thanksgiving," Chef Claire said.

"Good name," I said, nodding. "Because that's exactly what they are. I swear that one bite reminded me of Thanksgiving dinners from years ago."

"How is this possible?" Josie said, reaching for another.

Chef Claire grabbed one of the one-bite wonders and carefully cut it in half.

"I made a Chinese dumpling dough, and then I layered a thin slice of turkey, stuffing, mashed and sweet potatoes, and cranberry, then put a dollop of gravy over the top and sealed them tight. I did these on the stovetop, but I have another batch steaming at the moment."

I picked up one of the halves and examined it carefully. How it was possible to recreate an entire holiday dinner in an object that was less than an inch high was beyond my comprehension abilities, but I certainly wasn't going to argue the point.

I decided to postpone my earlier decision about being turkeyed out for another day and helped myself to another. Just as I was reaching for my fifth one, my phone rang. I wiped my hands and mouth and answered the call.

"This is Suzy. A delivery at this time of night?" I looked at Josie. She shook her head. "No, I'm sorry. I don't think we ordered anything for delivery tonight... What do you mean the contents are expiring?"

I frowned, and Josie sat back in her chair listening closely.

"Yes, I see... Who is this?"

The call ended abruptly, and I set my phone down on the table.

"That was odd," I said. "Whoever that was said there's been a delivery at the Inn and it's outside the door. And they said we should hurry up and get it because the contents are expiring."

"That is odd," Josie said. "It's so cold out there I can't imagine what could possibly spoil before morning."

"Yeah," I said, starting to reach for another of the appetizers. Then I stopped. "Unless it's alive."

"Like a dog," Josie said, scrambling to her feet.

We raced outside and headed down the stairs until we reached the back entrance of the Inn. There was nothing on the back porch, so we raced

3

around the side until we reached the front. Near the door was a cardboard box wrapped in a flimsy cotton blanket. Josie knelt down and pulled the blanket back. Tears immediately welled in my eyes when I heard the soft whimpers coming from inside the box.

I opened the front door and turned the thermostat way up as Josie carried the box into one of the examination rooms.

"This is bad," she said, carefully reaching into the box. "There are six of them. They can't be more than four weeks old."

"Can you save them?" I said.

"Well, we're certainly going to do everything we possibly can," Josie said. "Grab a bunch of blankets and towels."

She pulled out her phone and located the number.

"Sammy, it's Josie. I need you here now. Do you know where Jill is?...That's great. Bring her along. Get over here immediately."

She ended the call and refocused on what was inside the cardboard box. I returned with the blankets, and she spread them out one at a time on the floor and gently placed one of the puppies on a blanket and wrapped it loosely. She repeated the process until all six puppies were safely cocooned.

"Okay," she said. "Remember to remind Sammy and Jill when they get here that they can't rub or pet them until we're sure frostbite hasn't set in."

"But they all have some degree of hypothermia, right?"

"Yeah, let's hope that's as bad as it gets. But I'm worried about one of the front legs on the little guy on the left. He's showing signs of some serious tissue damage."

"You mean he might lose the leg?"

"It's a possibility, Suzy," she said. "But for now let's focus on making sure he doesn't lose his life. We need to deal with the hypothermia first."

I stared down at the dazed expressions on the cocker spaniel's faces and heard their whimpers as I continued to fight back the tears. A few minutes later, Sammy and Jill raced inside the exam room and glanced down at the six puppies wrapped in blankets on the floor.

"You got here fast," Josie said, cradling two of the puppies to her chest. "Both of you take a puppy and hold it like this."

Sammy and Jill each cradled a puppy, and I picked up the other two. I briefly outlined what had happened as the four of us sat on the tile floor and did our best to get the puppies' core temperature up.

"Thanks for coming in," I said.

"No problem," Sammy said, glancing at Jill. "We just happened to be watching a movie together tonight. I guess it was lucky that we were in the same place when you called."

Josie looked at me and grinned. Sammy and Jill had been seeing each other for at least three months, but they continued to believe that no one had figured that out yet. The main ingredient in a grilled cheese sandwich was a better-kept secret. This seemed like as good a time as any to pop that balloon.

"Sammy," I said.

"Yeah."

"We know."

"Know what?"

"About you and Jill," I said.

"You do?" Sammy said, glancing at Jill.

"I told you," Jill said, glancing nervously back and forth between Josie and me. "I'm sorry we didn't say anything. We weren't sure how you guys would react."

"Has your relationship impacted your work?" Josie said.

"No," Jill said.

"Or the way you treat the dogs?" Josie said.

"Absolutely not," Sammy said.

"Well, there you go," Josie said, glancing down at one of the puppies stirring in her arms. "This little guy is starting to come around. She's licking my hand."

"Mine too," I said.

Josie handed one of the dogs she was holding to Jill and stood, still holding the puppy with the damaged front leg close to her.

"Okay, I think it's safe to slowly remove the blankets," Josie said. "But if they start shivering again when you do, immediately wrap them back up. Suzy and Sammy, I need you to carefully check each puppy for potential frostbite. You're looking for signs of tissue discoloration, blisters, or swelling. And if they react in pain when you touch them, make a note of that area. If you find any of those symptoms, you'll need to run some warm water no hotter than 108 degrees and start by gently patting those spots with the water. Then wrap a dry, warm towel around them. If the spots look particularly damaged, go ahead and put a heating pad wrapped in a towel against it. But you can't rub or pet those spots the way you normally would. Pat, but don't rub. "

"Got it," I said, already pulling back one of the blankets to begin my examination. Then I glanced up at Josie. "Where are you going to be?"

"Surgery," Josie whispered. "I'm going to need your help, Jill."

Jill gently set the puppy she was holding down next to Sammy and stood. She followed Josie out of the exam room and headed for the back of the Inn where our surgery area was located. I knew what that meant and felt another round of tears streaming down my cheeks.

"What kind of monster leaves a litter of puppies outside in a box on a cold night like this?" Sammy said, gently rolling one of the puppies over onto its back.

"Actually, Sammy. I think whoever did this was trying to figure out a way to save them," I said.

Sammy thought about what I said for a moment, then refocused on the puppy he was examining.

"But why would they do it anonymously?" he said.

"Now that's a very good question."

Chapter 2

I yawned and almost nodded off sitting in the chair behind my desk. I sat up straight, startling myself when my head fell forward, and I almost dropped the cup of coffee I was holding. Sammy was sitting on the couch with Jill draped across his lap. They looked very comfortable and were both snoring softly. We'd been going all night, and it looked like our efforts were going to pay off.

Josie entered carrying her own cup of coffee and sat down in the chair across from me. She looked worn out but had a small smile on her face. She'd never admit it, but I knew she was proud of herself for saving the lives of the six puppies. Five of them were huddled together sleeping on a thick bed of blankets near the heating vent. The other puppy was still recovering from its surgery.

"I hated having to do that," Josie said, reaching for the candy jar sitting on top of the desk. "The poor little guy."

"He's going to be okay, right?"

"Yeah, I think so," she said, unwrapping a piece of chocolate. "We'll need to keep a close eye out for infection, but other than that I think he's going to make it."

"I've seen lots of dogs who manage to get around pretty well on three legs," I said.

"Sure," Josie said, nodding. "But it'll take him a while to get used to it and find his balance."

"We're going to keep him, Josie," I said.

"I was thinking the same thing," she said, reaching across the desk to pat my hand.

Again, I fought back another round of waterworks.

"You did good," Josie said. "And so did those two."

I glanced at Sammy and Jill who continued napping on the couch.

"We're going to have to come up with a good name for him," Josie said.

"How about Lucky?"

"Well, he's certainly that," Josie said, unpeeling another chocolate. "How about Trey or Triangle?"

"Nah, we can do better than that," I said.

"Wobble? No, I've got it. How about Tippy?"

"No, that seems cruel. We wouldn't want all the other dogs making fun of him," I said.

Josie raised an eyebrow at me.

"No, we wouldn't want that," she said, laughing. "You should probably head up to the house and get some sleep. You're starting to lose it."

"I'm fine," I said, yawning. "How about Tripod?"

"That's good," Josie said, nodding. "It calls out his unique quality without making fun of it. I like it."

"Okay, Tripod it is," I said. "What time is it anyway?"

"Six-thirty. Hey, Romeo and Juliet, wake up."

She nudged Sammy's leg with her foot. Sammy and Jill both stirred, then Jill sat up on the couch blinking.

"Good morning," Jill said, rubbing her eyes.

"You were snoring," I said, getting up to pour coffee for everyone.

"Sorry about that," Sammy said.

"I wasn't talking to you," I said, laughing.

Jill seemed too tired to worry about it and leaned back and tucked her head against Sammy's shoulder.

9

"We need to talk about a schedule for the next week," Josie said. "These guys are going to need a lot of attention."

"Let's hope giving them a bath is at the top of the list," Sammy said. "They stink really bad."

"Yes, they do," Josie said. "We should be able to take care of that this afternoon as soon as I'm sure they're out of danger."

"Puppies usually don't smell like that," Sammy said. "They usually smell like, well, puppies."

Sometimes it was hard to argue with Sammy's logic. And this time, I was simply too tired to try.

"They're from a puppy mill," I said. "That's the smell of abuse and neglect."

Josie nodded and took a sip of coffee.

"I've never heard of anybody operating a puppy mill around here," Sammy said.

"That's because Suzy and Josie would hunt them down if they were," Jill said, laughing.

There was no reason to argue with Jill's logic. We would. And it looked like we might be forced to do just that.

"A lot of those mills don't sell in the same location where the dogs are bred," I said. "The dogs are often sold in different towns or even other states."

"We'll deal with those people later," Josie said. "For now, we need to focus on the puppies. It looks like they're about a month old."

"Dogs don't start weaning until after five or six weeks, right?" Sammy said.

"Correct," Josie said. "That means they'll need at least another week of hand feeding. Jill, can you make sure we have lots of the powdered milk supplement on hand?"

"You got it," Jill said.

"They'll need to be fed four times a day," Josie said. "Let's go seven, eleven, three, and seven. And if necessary, we'll add a fifth late night feeding. They're pretty malnourished at the moment, so I'd rather overfeed a bit for the next several days than the other way around."

"I think we should keep them together in one of the condos down here during the day, and then we can take them up to the house at night to keep an eye on them," I said.

Josie nodded, then glanced at Sammy when he cleared his throat.

"You think it's a good idea to keep moving them back and forth every day?" he said.

"We can't leave them alone all night," I said. "I may be a bit of a fanatic when it comes to taking care of our dogs, but I'm certainly not sleeping down here."

"Yeah, you have to draw the line somewhere," Josie said, laughing.

"I'll do it," Sammy said.

"What?" I said.

"I'd like to do it," Sammy said. "They need our help. And I'm still the most junior person on staff, so it should be me."

"Sammy, you don't have to do that," Josie said. "That's way above and beyond the call of duty."

"No, I insist," he said. "Besides, I've been thinking about adopting a dog. Maybe one of them will pick me."

"Sammy, if you spend a couple of weeks with them around the clock, you may end up having to take all six," I said, laughing.

"Worse things could happen," he said, shrugging.

I couldn't argue with his logic on that one. Despite his need for sleep, the kid was on his game.

"Okay," Josie said. "Why don't you head home for the rest of the day, get your stuff ready, and be back here for the seven o'clock feeding?"

Sammy got up off the couch, kissed Jill on the top of the head and left the office. Jill stretched back out on the couch.

"I'm just going to catch a quick nap, and then I'll handle reception the rest of the day. The schedule is really light this week," Jill said. "Or at least it was."

"Sounds good. Thanks, Jill," I said, yawning. "I think I'll head up to the house, grab a shower and then be back in about an hour."

"That works," Josie said. "I'll keep an eye on things here. Bring snacks."

I snorted and shook my head. But I knew that Josie wouldn't be going anywhere for the next several hours until she was certain she'd done everything possible to make sure the puppies were safe and comfortable. The least I could do was make sure she was fed. Then Josie caught my eye and winked.

"Oh, Jill," Josie said.

"Yeah?" Jill said, not even bothering to open her eyes.

"I know you'll be helping Sammy out and I want to thank you in advance for doing that," Josie said.

"It's not a problem," Jill said, yawning.

"And Jill?"

"Yeah?"

"I know that might involve some long hours for both of you," Josie said, grinning.

"So?" Jill said, opening her eyes and turning her head to look at Josie.

"So just remember that our visitation hours end at ten," Josie deadpanned.

"Funny," Jill said, shutting her eyes.

We did a quick check on the puppies that were huddled close and sleeping comfortably and walked outside into the reception area. Josie noticed me fiddling with my phone and a pen.

"What are you doing?" she said, leaning against the reception counter.

"Jotting down the number of that call from last night," I said, writing on my hand.

"You're going to call Jackson, aren't you?" Josie said.

"I certainly am. I'm sure our Chief of Police won't mind helping us identify the number. With any luck, we'll know who we need to have a little chat with by the end of the day."

"Us?" Josie said.

"Absolutely," I said. "This one's personal."

"Okay. That's what I was afraid of. But I'll need to eat, shower, and sleep first. In that order."

"Sure," I said as I started to head for the back door.

Then I stopped and turned around. Josie didn't seem surprised by my move at all. In fact, from the expression on her face, it looked like she'd been expecting it.

"Yes," she said, staring back at me.

"We're going to take these guys down, Josie. I'm making it my personal mission."

"I'd expect nothing less from you."

Chapter 3

I stared down at the steaming bowl of penne and did my best to remain patient until Chef Claire and Josie got settled at the table. After my mother's comments about my lack of table manners, I was getting an early start on a New Year's resolution to be a more refined eater. I was also considering a resolution about cutting back on my overall food consumption, but I hadn't made a final decision on that one. Before I commit to anything drastic on that front, I'll see how well I survive Chef Claire's holiday menus and our upcoming round of Christmas parties.

"The things some people will do for money," Chef Claire said, taking a bite of her latest masterpiece. "I mean, really. Who could do that to a litter of puppies?"

"The sad fact is that there are probably more of them out there," Josie said.

"But we're going to find them," I said, nibbling on a piece of penne.

Josie chewed as she watched my slow and deliberate movements.

"Could you please pass the parmesan, Chef Claire?" I said, setting my fork down on my plate.

Chef Claire glanced at the cheese that was a relatively easy reach for me but nodded and slid the bowl of cheese directly in front of me. She glanced at Josie, who continued to eat her dinner and stare at me. Chef Claire shrugged and went back to her dinner.

"Thank you," I said, slowly spreading a spoonful of parmesan over my pasta.

I forked a single piece of pasta into my mouth, chewed slowly, and then wiped my mouth with a napkin.

"What are you doing?" Josie said, raising an eyebrow at me.

"I'm eating my dinner," I said, spearing another piece of penne. "What does it look like I'm doing?"

"A bad impression of a charm school dropout," Josie said, laughing.

"Funny," I said, again selecting and chewing a single piece of pasta.

"Well, whatever you're doing, stop it," Josie said, reaching for a slice of garlic bread. "You're freaking me out."

"You're right," I said. "Who am I kidding?"

I stuffed half a meatball into my mouth and grabbed a piece of garlic bread.

I'm glad I got an early start on this resolution. It was going be a lot harder than I thought.

My phone buzzed. Recognizing the number, I put the phone on speaker and placed it on the kitchen table.

"Hey, Jackson," I said.

"Hey, Suzy," Jackson said. "The connection sounds scratchy."

"No, that's just Josie," I said, laughing. "She's eating."

"Oh, for a moment there, I thought I heard artillery fire."

"Funny," Josie mumbled through a mouthful of garlic bread.

"Did you have any luck tracking down that number?" I said.

"Yeah, it was easy," Jackson said. "What are you guys having for dinner?"

"A tomato-basil penne, meatballs, garlic bread, and a garden salad with a vinaigrette I'm thinking about using as a cologne," I said.

"Aren't you sweet," Chef Claire said, laughing. "Hey, Jackson, I made plenty if you'd like to join us."

All three of us jumped when we heard the kitchen door open. Jackson stepped inside still holding the phone to his ear.

"Don't mind if I do," he said, sliding his phone into his pocket and sitting down next to me. "I was just in the neighborhood."

"Unbelievable," Josie said, getting up from the table to grab a plate and bowl for Jackson.

Chef Claire poured him a glass of wine, and I studied the two of them closely. Both Jackson and our local medical examiner, Freddie, had recently embarked on their own individual campaigns to win Chef Claire's affections. So far, neither one had gotten any traction, but Josie and I were having a ball egging both men on. I made a mental note to tell Freddie about Jackson's surprise dinner appearance the next time I saw him.

Jackson took a bite of salad and sighed. Then he sampled the penne and murmured. By the time he got halfway through his first meatball, he was talking to himself and staring off into the distance.

"Earth to Jackson," I said. "The phone number?"

"Oh, yeah," Jackson said, wiping his mouth. "I almost forgot. It's a payphone."

"A payphone?" I said, glancing at Josie. "They still have those things?"

"I can't remember the last time I saw a payphone. Or one of those see through phone booths," Josie said.

"They're still around," Jackson said. "But their numbers are way down. This one is at the old general store in Wildwood."

Wildwood was a tiny farming town about ten miles from Clay Bay. The general store Jackson was referring to had closed several years ago, as had pretty much every other business that used to line its main street. About the only thing there these days were some small family farms, a couple of fast food joints, and a dive bar called the Outer Limit. I'd been there a couple times when I was younger, and it hadn't taken me long to decide it was aptly named.

"That store has been closed for years," I said. "I'm surprised the phone is still working."

"Yeah, I was too," Jackson said. "But I guess it's good to have it there in case of an emergency. Speaking of emergencies, how are the puppies doing?"

"They're all going to make it," I said. "Thanks to Josie."

Josie blushed as she reached for the salad bowl.

"Have you ever heard of any puppy mills in the area?" I said.

"No," he said, shaking his head. "And I asked around with the state police and some of the other local cops in the area, but nobody's ever heard of anything like that operating around here."

"Well, we've got one now," I said.

"Maybe," Jackson said. "It might have just been a family that didn't know what else to do with a litter of puppies."

"No," Josie said, shaking her head. "Those little guys were from a puppy mill. I'm sure of it."

"How do these mills operate?" Chef Claire said. "I've heard the term, but never the details."

"Oh, the people who run them are simply wonderful human beings," Josie said, spearing a meatball with her fork. "Most of the mills are unlicensed and can house hundreds of dogs that are kept in deplorable conditions. The females are constantly being bred without adequate time to recover between litters. And when they become physically worn out and unable to reproduce, they're often killed. The conditions are unsanitary, crowded, and the dogs are usually housed in cages that are often stacked on top of each other. No fresh air, no toys or exercise, not enough food and water."

Josie paused and gripped the edge of the kitchen table with both hands. Tears formed in the corners of her eyes, and she took several deep breaths.

17

"Should I continue?" she whispered.

"No, I got it," Chef Claire said, staring at Josie. "How about some dessert?"

"Maybe later," Josie said as she got up from the table and left the kitchen.

"Wow," Chef Claire said. "That was intense. I'd hate to be one of those guys if you two got your hands on them."

"When we get our hands on them," I said.

"Please don't do anything crazy, Suzy," Jackson said.

"There's nothing crazy about making sure people like that get what's coming to them, is there, Jackson?"

"No, I guess not," Jackson said. "But just try to keep me in the loop, okay?"

"Okay," I said, nodding, then glancing at Chef Claire. "Did I hear you mention something about dessert?"

Chef Claire laughed and headed for the fridge. She returned carrying a tray just as Josie reentered the kitchen. She was drying her face with a hand towel, and she sat back down and glanced around the table.

"Sorry about that," Josie said. "Those mills are a real sore point with me. What did I miss?"

"Not a thing," Chef Claire said, removing the foil from the tray.

"Cannoli," I whispered.

"Yes, chocolate-almond," Chef Claire said.

"With the Amaretto cream filling?" Josie said.

"That's the one," Chef Claire said. "Think you could force a couple down?"

Josie shrugged.

"I could eat."

Chapter 4

We waited until Jackson made his reluctant, schoolboy departure, then hopped in my SUV to make the short drive to Wildwood. The straight two-lane county highway was empty except for the occasional patch of drifting snow accumulating along the side of the road. The full moon illuminated the flat, snow-covered fields that dominated the landscape and it seemed to sparkle in the moonlight.

"It's beautiful," Josie said, staring out the window.

"Yeah, as long as we're inside a warm car," I said. "But imagine what's it like to be a dog in a cage stashed away in a shed or a cold barn."

"I've been trying not to," Josie snapped. "But thanks for the reminder."

"Sorry," I said, gripping the wheel tighter. "I can't tell you how much I want to hurt these people."

"I know."

I made a right turn onto a small road that soon became Main Street. Since it appeared to be the only street in sight, it had obviously been correctly named. This end of town was dark and empty. Several hundred yards ahead I could see a glimmer of neon I knew was the sign for the Outer Limit.

"It's spooky," Josie said, glancing around. "I guess if I wanted to do something illegal, this would be a good place to do it."

I nodded and came to a stop in front of an empty, rundown building with boarded windows. A faded sign that read Wildwood General Store was suspended off the front of the building, and it creaked softly as it swung back and forth in the breeze. I grabbed my flashlight, and we hopped out of the car and stood on the street looking for signs of the payphone.

"It must be on the side somewhere," I said, walking toward the corner of the building.

Josie followed, and we reached the edge of the building and started walking down an unshoveled path.

"I guess they don't have much of a budget for keeping the streets shoveled," Josie said.

"Or street lights," I said, turning on the flashlight. "I think I see it up there on the right."

The only sound we heard was the snow crunching under our boots. It was a cold night, but we were dressed for it, and I was actually enjoying being outside until we reached the phone booth. It was one of the see-through models with one door that folded in half to open and close. Right now, the door was wedged open because the body with a single bullet wound in the middle of the forehead was sitting down with one leg extended at an odd angle preventing the door from closing.

"Oh, no," Josie said, recoiling at the sight of the frozen body with the confused look on his face. "Here we go again."

"Yeah. And all we wanted to do was take a look at the phone," I said, staring down at the dead man. "The phone's off the hook. Do you think it's possible he was still on the phone with us when he got shot?"

"I guess anything is possible," Josie said. "You said the call ended abruptly, but you didn't hear a gunshot."

"Whoever shot him could have used a silencer," I said.

"Yeah, sure," Josie said, glancing around. "But why bother? From the looks of the place, you could set off fireworks and not have anybody hear it."

I nodded in agreement and called Jackson.

"Hey, Jackson."

"Hi, Suzy. Thanks again for dinner. As always, it was amazing. And I think I made some more progress with Chef Claire."

"Good for you," I said, changing ears to block the wind. "Look, Jackson, we hate to do this, but you and Freddie need to get out here. And you might as well bring the state police with you."

"What have you done, Suzy?"

"We haven't done anything, Jackson. And I don't think I like your tone."

"Well, excuse me," he said. "What's going on?"

I explained where we were and told him about the dead body. Jackson listened closely, reminded us to stay there and not touch anything, then hung up.

"He's on his way," I said.

"We need to wait here, right?" Josie said, bouncing up and down on her toes.

"I guess we can wait in the car."

I turned around and took a couple of steps before coming to an abrupt stop. Josie was hunched down against the wind and walked straight into me.

"What are you waiting for?" she said.

"Hang on," I said, heading toward the dead body in the phone booth.

"Suzy, don't do it," Josie said, her voice rising.

I ignored her warning and knelt down over the dead man. I located his wallet and pulled it out. I held the flashlight up for Josie.

"Sure," she said, taking the flashlight from me. "Make me an accomplice."

"Relax," I said, going through the contents of the wallet. "Eat one of your cannoli."

"I left them in the car," she said. "How did you know I brought some?"

"Lucky guess," I said, removing the man's driver license. "Jerome Jefferson. The address is somewhere in Albany."

"Okay, we know his name and where he lived," Josie said. "Let's go before you end up committing a felony."

"Hang on," I said, unfolding a piece of paper with an address written on it. "This must be someplace local."

I scribbled the information on my hand, folded the piece of paper and put it back in the wallet along with the man's license. I slid the wallet back into the dead man's pocket and stood up. My back and knees ached in protest, and my breathing was labored.

"I so need to get to the gym," I said, heading down the path back toward the car.

"Maybe Santa will bring you a gym membership for Christmas," Josie said.

"You didn't, did you?" I said, glancing back at her.

Josie snorted.

"That is not one of your better qualities," I said, picking up my pace.

"Probably not," she said, laughing. "But it certainly is effective."

She jogged past me and easily beat me to the car.

"C'mon, slowpoke. It's freezing out here."

We climbed in the car, and I started it and turned the heater up. I tried to catch my breath then felt Josie nudge my shoulder. I glanced over at the cannoli she was holding.

"Thanks," I said, savoring the first bite. "You know, if I felt half as good working out as this cannoli makes me feel, I'd never leave the gym."

"Maybe you should start with walking. You know, like walking out of the kitchen," Josie said, laughing.

"You're one to talk," I said, reaching for another cannoli.

Then I saw the lights of three cars heading toward us.

"There they are," I said, turning the car off and getting out.

We greeted Jackson, Freddie, and Detective Abrams from the state police.

"Ladies," Freddie said, stamping snow off his boots. "We really need to stop meeting like this."

"Did you save me a cannoli?" Jackson said, laughing.

"Sorry. They're all gone," Josie said.

"How did you know they had cannoli?" Freddie said, staring at Jackson.

"I was at their place for dinner tonight," Jackson said.

"What?" Freddie said. "Was Chef Claire there?"

"Of course."

Freddie wasn't pleased by the news and he stamped his feet again. Not much snow came off his boots this time.

"Hey, Detective Abrams," I said. "How's Wally doing?"

Wally was the detective's basset hound we took care of whenever he needed vet care or boarding.

"He's great," Detective Abrams said. "He's going to be four tomorrow. My wife, of course, is throwing a party for him."

I laughed, then waited for him to turn all business as he always did.

"Would you mind telling me why I'm here standing in the cold at this time of night?" Detective Abrams said.

"There's a dead body in the phone booth around back," I said, leading the way.

"Do you know who it is?" Jackson said.

"No, I've never seen him before," I said, glancing at Josie.

That was true. I hadn't. But I decided not to divulge the fact that I'd gone through the man's wallet. Judging from the looks on their faces, they hadn't needed to ask.

Some people just have no faith in others.

The three men huddled around the phone booth and stared down at the body.

"One in the forehead," Freddie said. "And judging from the condition, my guess is that he's been out here in the cold for at least a day."

"Jackson told me that someone called you from this number last night around nine," Detective Abrams said.

Josie and I retold the story about the call and the subsequent discovery of the box of puppies on our front steps. Detective Abrams and Freddie listened closely while Jackson, who had heard the story before, knelt down over the body and started going through his pockets.

"He had a Syracuse address," Jackson said, reading from the driver license.

"Albany," I said without thinking.

Jackson shook his head and laughed.

"You're unbelievable," he said, handing the license to Detective Abrams.

"Oops," I said, embarrassed at being caught red-handed.

"Smooth," Josie whispered.

Jackson unfolded the piece of paper I'd found earlier.

"It looks like an address of some sort," he said, studying it. "But these look like map coordinates."

Detective Abrams examined the piece of paper and nodded.

"Should be easy enough to find with GPS," he said, then turned to us. "Okay, thanks for calling it in. But there's no reason for you two to stick around. Why don't you just head on home and get some sleep while Freddie starts working his magic?"

"That's a very good idea," Josie said, glancing at me.

I shrugged and snuck a peek at what was written on my hand. Josie caught it and even in the dim light I could tell she was scowling at me. We waved our goodbyes and headed back to the car.

"You want me to punch those coordinates into my phone, don't you?" Josie said.

"Yes."

I started the car and unzipped my coat.

"We don't have any choice," Josie said, tapping the touchscreen.

"No, if it's the location of a puppy mill, we need to know tonight," I said.

"Should we tell them where we're going?" Josie said.

"I'd rather not," I said. "You know how Jackson always reacts when we start poking around."

"Okay," Josie said.

"That's it?" I said. "No complaining, no trying to talk me out of it?

"No. Not this time. Somebody's messing with the safety and wellbeing of dogs. There's nothing to discuss."

I reached over and squeezed her arm as I drove along the empty street. When the street met the highway, I waited for Josie's instructions. Moments later, she glanced up from her phone and pointed right.

Chapter 5

The coordinates Josie entered into her phone revealed a location that I must have driven past dozens of times during my youth when my friends and I would borrow one of our parent's car and cruise the desolate back roads, especially during the time of year when it wasn't possible to be on the River. Following her instructions, I turned off the small two-lane road onto an even smaller dirt road that led us through a thick stand of pine trees and various rock formations until we reached a small farmhouse and a barn. Both structures appeared to be deserted, and when I turned the car lights off, we were surrounded by total darkness.

We grabbed our flashlights and headed for the house to confirm our suspicions that the place was empty. Since our major concern was what we might find in the barn, as soon as we were sure no one was in the house, we headed for the dilapidated structure about a hundred yards from the house. As soon as we slid the door back, we heard barking and the sound of whimpering. I found a light switch, and we both recoiled when we saw the cages and the filthy conditions.

Josie immediately dialed a number on her phone.

"Sammy," Josie said. "Is Jill there with you? Good. Look, I need you to bring the van to the location I'm going to give you... Yes, we found more... I'm not sure how many yet. Grab a bunch of blankets and towels. Make sure Jill is okay watching the spaniel pups and get out here as soon as you can. And bring my bag and some of those dog treats with the supplements. Thanks."

She ended the call and dialed another.

"Jackson, it's Josie. Look, we've found the puppy mill, and we're going to need some help transporting some dogs back to the Inn…Sammy's bringing our van out, but if you could organize a couple people with either a truck or van and get out here that would be great."

Josie confirmed the coordinates with him along with a description of where we'd turned off the road and hung up. She joined me near a stack of cages where I was desperately trying to figure out where to begin.

"How many do you think there are?" she said, shaking her head in disgust.

"It looks like a couple dozen. And that includes two litters of lab puppies. If there's anything that even comes close to good news here, it looks like they were a bit low on inventory at the moment," I said.

"Or they took the rest of the dogs with them when they left," Josie said, kneeling down to open the cage of a female lab that stared up at us with a sad, tired expression. "How you doing, girl? Hang in there."

"I'll get them some water," I said.

I collected a handful of filthy bowls that were scattered on the dirt floor of the barn and grabbed the hose that was hanging on a wall. I did my best to wash the bowls, then filled them and placed them on the floor where the dogs were huddled around Josie. The water was a big hit and, except for one, they were all very happy to see us. A scrawny male lab stood in the back of its now open cage cowering and snarling at us. I approached his cage.

"Be careful, Suzy," Josie said. "If you get bit, you could be looking at a serious round of rabies shots."

"I know," I said, sitting down in front of the dog's cage.

He continued to snarl and started snapping his jaws at me.

"He's scared to death," Josie said as she stroked the head of one of the adult females.

27

"Yeah. And sick and tired of being abused," I said, holding out a dog biscuit.

The dog sniffed the air, then resumed his throaty growl. I tossed the biscuit in front of him, and he snatched it and wolfed it down. I repeated the process. On the fifth biscuit, he took a step toward me and took one from my hand. Five minutes later, I'd convinced him we were old friends. I stood, and he finally worked his way out of his cage. I say worked because he wasn't walking very well.

Jackson, coming directly from the murder scene, was the first to arrive. He entered the barn, took a look around, and shook his head.

"At times like these I'm ashamed to call myself human," Jackson said. "I can't believe the people who did this come from the same species as me."

He walked toward us, and the male lab went into a barking frenzy. Jackson stopped in his tracks and stared at the dog.

"You might want to keep your distance from this guy, Jackson," I said. "It looks like he might have some issues with men."

"Yeah, I got that, Suzy," Jackson said, moving closer to Josie. "What do you need me to do?"

"If you could take the three adult females in your car back to the Inn that would be great," Josie said. "There are two labs and a German Shepherd. They're in pretty rough shape and are going to need some work. And you'll probably need to carry them to your car. But they all seem friendly and shouldn't give you any trouble."

"You got it," Jackson said, kneeling down to pet one of the female labs.

A few minutes later Sammy arrived. Five minutes after that, two of Jackson's friends pulled their vehicles next to the barn. Fifteen minutes later, all twenty-five dogs were on their way to the Inn. Twenty minutes after that, Josie and I were in the back of the Inn with Sammy and Jill deciding how we were going to assign the dogs to one of the condos.

"Well, the litters of puppies and their mamas each get a condo," Josie said. "Jill, can you get them settled in?"

"You got it, Josie," Jill said, grabbing a stack of blankets.

"Sammy, can you take the German Shepherd into one of the exam rooms?" Josie said.

"Sure. What do you think's wrong with her?" Sammy said, stroking the dog's head.

"Do you see her stomach?"

"Yeah, she looks like she just ate a big meal but I know that didn't happen," Sammy said.

"She's pregnant," Josie said. "Suzy, I need to take a look at her. Can you handle the rest of this?"

"Sure," I said.

"After I make sure the German Shepherd is okay, I need to take a look at the male lab with the hip problem. Then I'm going to examine all the puppies. But if you come across any others that look like they need immediate care, come get me."

Josie headed off, and I went back to figuring out how we were going to accommodate all of our new guests. By the time I finished, the dogs were all fed and watered, and the Inn was at full capacity.

By the time midnight rolled around, Josie and I were finally able to take a break. I was sitting behind my desk, and Josie was sprawled out on the couch drifting off to sleep when Chef Claire entered carrying a picnic basket. We both perked up immediately.

"You're so good," I said.

"I figured you'd be hungry," Chef Claire said, removing a hot tray of lasagna from the basket.

"Unbelievable," Josie said, staring at the wedge of lasagna Chef Claire cut for her.

Jackson poked his head into the office.

"I thought I smelled Italian," he said, sitting down.

"If you ever wash out as a cop, Jackson, you've got a bright future as a stalker," I said, laughing.

"I'll keep that in mind," he said, grinning at Chef Claire. "How are they all doing?"

"It looks like they're all going to make it. The male lab might need surgery if I can't get him walking pain-free," Josie said.

"What happened to him?" Jackson said, accepting a plate of food from Chef Claire.

"He's probably been kicked," Josie said, her eyes dark with rage. "And more than once."

"If I ever got my hands on whoever did this, I might have to forget that I'm a cop for a while," Jackson said. "You don't do those things to a defenseless animal."

"Not if you expect to call yourself a human being you don't," Josie said. "I was worried about a couple of the puppies, but once I got some fluids in them, they perked up."

"How long do you think they would have lasted in that barn?" Jackson said, taking a bite of lasagna.

"It's hard to say," Josie said. "A couple of days, maybe a week."

"That would have been a horrible way for them to die," he said.

"Yeah, not to mention the horrible way they had to live," I said. "What's the deal with that house?"

"That's the old Wilkerson house," Jackson said. "The family moved south a few years ago, and the place has been empty. At least that's what everyone thought. We're trying to track the family down in Florida to see if they've been renting it out."

I picked a long string of cheese off the side of my face. I had no idea how I'd managed to miss my mouth by that much. My table manners resolution was apparently going to need my undivided attention.

"What about the dead guy?" I said, ignoring Josie who was laughing at my battle with the cheese.

"You mean Jerome Jefferson from Albany?" Jackson deadpanned.

I made a face and stuck my tongue out at him.

"Yeah, that's the one," I said.

"Jerome, as we say in the business, was your basic waste of oxygen," Jackson said. "Multiple counts of breaking and entering, stolen cars, all the usual suspects. And he was part of a gang that was knocking off fast food joints around Albany a couple years ago. He got caught when he went back to the place they'd just robbed."

"Went back?" I said.

"Yeah," Jackson said, laughing. "They got his order wrong. They forgot his fries."

"I hate when that happens," Josie said.

"Apparently so did Jerome," Jackson said. "But before he could have a little chat with the manager, he walked right into two state cops on his way back in. He did a year, got paroled, and then the cops in Albany lost track of him. Which makes sense since he was probably living up here."

"Did he have any history with puppy mills?" I said.

"Not that we can tell yet," Jackson said. "But it's still early."

"We're going to find these people, Jackson," I said.

"Yeah, I was expecting you to say that," he said. "And I know that nothing I do or say is going to change your mind, but just promise me you guys won't do anything crazy."

"Jackson, you have our word that we'll be the perfect citizens you expect us to be," I said. "We're just going to add one new role for the time being."

"Unhinged vigilante?" he said.

"Exactly," I said.

Josie polished off the last of her lasagna, then looked up from her plate and nodded at Jackson.

"What she said."

Chapter 6

The news about the murder and our discovery of the puppy mill spread through town like soft butter on a hot roll. Several locals, including a group of high school students who had done internships with us, dropped by the Inn to volunteer their help, or to check out the dogs that would soon be available for adoption. We were amazed by the immense level of community support we received, and I was more puffed with pride than a marshmallow in a microwave.

And if I didn't eat lunch soon, the number of labored food analogies that were creeping into my brain would soon be off the charts. I tapped the horn, and Josie trotted down the driveway in the direction of the SUV. She climbed in the passenger seat, and we headed for town.

"You're late," I said.

"Sally Beauchamp stopped by to adopt two of the lab puppies. She was taking her time deciding which two she wanted."

"That's a tough decision," I said. "It's like trying to decide between Chef Claire's chocolate-almond and pistachio-cream cannoli."

Josie shook her head.

"How long have you been making the food analogies?" she said.

"About an hour," I said, feeling my stomach rumble.

"Let's get some food into you," Josie said. "Don't forget we need to swing by and pick up Chef Claire."

"I hope she's ready."

I stopped in front of a large stone building and parked next to my mother's new Audi. She'd recently been given the car by her former boyfriend, a car dealer who'd been caught cheating on her. My mother likes to call the car a parting gift. I think she extorted it from the smarmy creature, but we've agreed to disagree on that one. Mom swaps out her cars more often than most restaurants change the cooking oil in their fryers, but I have a feeling she might keep this one around for a while.

I really need to eat.

We walked inside and found Chef Claire and my mother talking with the architect who had just completed the design plans for the new restaurant we were opening with Chef Claire. They were staring down at the blueprints that were spread across a makeshift table comprised of an old door and two stools. Chef Claire and my mother were staring down at the plans and nodding as the architect talked and pointed at various spots. I glanced over my mother's shoulder and listened, then nodded.

When in Rome, right?

"Are you ready?" I said to Chef Claire.

"Oh, hi. I didn't even hear you two come in," Chef Claire said. "Let me grab my coat."

"Hi, Mom," I said, giving her a kiss on the cheek.

"Hello, darling," she said, giving me a quick once-over. "Josie, you're looking beautiful as always."

"Thanks, Mrs. C.," Josie said, hugging her. "How do the plans look?"

"They are simply amazing," my mother said. "Suzy, Josie, I'd like you to meet Ray Waterbury, architect extraordinaire."

"Nice to meet you, ladies," Ray said, his eyes lingering on Josie. "I think you're really going to like what we're doing here."

"We can't wait," I said, glancing over my shoulder to see what was taking Chef Claire so long to find her coat. "Would you two like to join us for lunch, Mom?"

"Oh, I'd love to, darling, but Ray and I already have plans," she said, laughing. "And if we were all at the same table, I wouldn't be able to tell all my juicy stories about you behind your back, would I?"

"I wouldn't believe too much of what comes out of my mother's mouth, Ray. She's a drinker."

"Funny, darling."

I hugged her again, and we headed for the door where Chef Claire was waiting for us. She was wearing a parka, wool cap, gloves, and a thick scarf wrapped and tied tight around her neck.

"Think you'll be warm enough?" Josie deadpanned, nodding at her ensemble.

"Hey, it's freezing out there," Chef Claire said.

"It's not even officially winter yet," Josie said.

"Tell that to my feet."

"C'mon, let's go," I said. "If you guys are going to argue, at least do it from the comfort of a warm restaurant."

We climbed in the SUV and made the short drive to the Water's Edge. The owner, Millie, and her German Shepherd, Barkley, greeted us at the door.

"Hi, folks," Millie said. "Where's Chloe, Suzy?"

Chloe was my Australian shepherd that Josie and I had rescued from the River one early morning about six months earlier. I understood why Millie asked the question; Chloe and I were inseparable.

"When I left the house, she was stretched out in front of the fire," I said.

"Smart dog," Chef Claire said, removing her gloves and heading for a table in the back near the fireplace.

"She's helping Sammy keep an eye on a litter of puppies," I said, reaching down to greet Barkley.

"Yeah, I heard about that puppy mill," Millie said. "Who could do something like that?"

"Someone with a death wish," Josie said, picking up a menu, scanning it briefly, then setting it down.

"You know, I've been thinking about getting another dog to keep Barkley company," Millie said.

"If you're looking for another German Shepherd, we're going to have a litter pretty soon," Josie said.

"Really?" Millie said, wiping down the table. "I may just have to take one of those off your hands."

"Take two," Josie said, laughing. "They're small."

"Yeah, but they don't stay that way very long, do they?"

"No, they certainly don't. Okay, I'm ready to order," Josie said.

"Let me guess," Millie said, laughing. "French onion soup, cheeseburger, the combo of fries and onion rings, and a slice of coconut cream pie for dessert."

"I told you she was clairvoyant," Josie said, glancing at me.

I laughed, glanced at Chef Claire who nodded, and I held up three fingers at Millie.

"You got it," Millie said. "What would you like to drink?"

We all ordered coffee and water and settled in.

"What's this guy Ray like?" I said.

"He seems nice, and I think your mom kind of likes him," Chef Claire said.

"Kind of likes him? So he's definitely not a keeper, huh?" I said.

"No. Ray's definitely catch and release," Chef Claire said.

We all laughed. My mother's dating philosophy often reminded me of fast food. At first, you felt satisfied, but soon you felt a lump in the pit of your stomach and left you wishing you'd made a smarter choice.

Another food analogy?

Man, I was heading south in a hurry.

What's keeping my French onion soup?

"How do you suggest we get started?" Josie said.

"I usually work my way through the cheese and the croutons first," I said, staring into the roaring fire.

"What on earth are you talking about?" Josie said, staring at me.

"Oh, you meant getting started finding out who was operating the puppy mill," I said, refocusing on my lunch companions. "Sorry about that."

Millie approached carrying a tray with three large bowls. She served us and headed back to the kitchen.

"So, Sherlock," Josie said, digging into her steaming bowl of soup. "What's the plan?"

"I have no idea," I said, starting my battle with another long string of melted mozzarella.

"This is really good," Chef Claire said.

I slurped a spoonful of soup and didn't spill a drop. Then something sitting on the table next to us caught my eye. I got up, grabbed the newspaper, and sat down.

"You're interrupting your lunch to read the newspaper?" Josie said, again staring at me.

"Hang on," I said, flipping to the classifieds. "Wouldn't this be a good place to start? People are always advertising dogs for sale in the paper."

"Actually, that's a really good idea," Josie said. "I'm impressed."

"Thanks. It's what I do."

I made it through my soup, then the rest of my lunch with one hand on my food, the other on the pen I used to circle various classified ads. By the time I was done, I was stuffed, and we had seven leads to start working on.

They weren't necessarily good leads, but they were better than doing nothing.

I paid for lunch, and the three of us headed back to the Inn. Chef Claire headed to the house while Josie and I checked in with our staff. The male lab with the bad hip seemed to be responding to Josie's treatments and was able to hop to his feet when he saw us enter the condos. The three adult females were starting to put weight on, and two of them seemed to be producing enough milk to feed their pups. But Josie instructed Sammy and Jill to maintain our hand feeding schedule for a few more days. We spent a couple of hours saying hello to all forty-seven dogs, then called it quits for the day and headed for the house.

After dinner, we started making calls to our seven leads ostensibly to enquire about purchasing a dog. Four of the leads turned out to be families whose dog had delivered a litter of pups. Two other leads were for legitimate local breeders we were familiar with. When I called the seventh number, I got a recorded message that the number was no longer in service.

I immediately called Jackson and gave him the number requesting him to track down the person who'd had it. He called back an hour later.

"Hey, Jackson," I said, putting the phone on speaker.

"What are you folks doing?" he said.

"Watching a movie, drinking wine, playing with the dogs, snacking," I said, grabbing a handful of parmesan-garlic popcorn. "You want to come over?"

"I'd love to, but I'm buried in this murder case at the moment."

"That's too bad," I said. "I'm sure Chef Claire would love to see you."

"Shut up, Suzy," Chef Claire said, grabbing the bowl of popcorn and setting it down out of my reach.

"Hey, that's not fair," I said, laughing.

Chef Claire grabbed a handful of popcorn and chewed it while staring at me.

Well played. Score a point for Chef Claire.

"I found the owner of that phone number," Jackson said.

"That's great," I said, reaching for my pen. "Who is it?"

"The recently deceased Jerome Jefferson."

"Really?"

"Yeah. So I guess that's the end of that trail," Jackson said.

"Yeah, it certainly looks that way," I said.

"Wait a minute," Josie said, her own bowl of popcorn tucked carefully in her lap. "How did Jerome the Dead manage to call the phone company to cancel his service after he caught one in the brainpan?"

"Caught one in the brainpan?" I said, staring at her. "Who are you?"

"I saw it on an old episode of Columbo and have been dying to work it into a conversation," Josie said. "Good one, huh?"

"No," I said. "And stop it."

Josie made a face at me and then turned to Jackson.

"My point is, if the number was in his name, how did it get disconnected so soon? More importantly, who told them to disconnect it?"

"I hate to say this," Jackson said. "But that's a very good question, Josie."

"Sometimes my brainpan has its moments," she said, tossing back another handful of popcorn.

"Is there any way you could find out who was paying the phone bill?" I said.

"As soon as I get off this call," Jackson said. "I should have already done that. I must be slipping."

"Unrequited lust will do that to you," I said, grinning at Chef Claire.

"Don't listen to her, Chef Claire," Jackson said. "Everybody knows she's unstable."

"So now you're saying you aren't interested in Chef Claire, Jackson?" Josie said.

Chef Claire snatched Josie's bowl of popcorn out of her lap and moved to the far end of the couch.

"Hey, you bring that back," Josie said.

Chef Claire made a point of eating from both bowls as she glared at us. She was definitely on her game tonight.

"I'll call you back as soon as I hear anything," Jackson said. "Or I could just swing by on my way home."

Chef Claire slowly shook her head back and forth and pointed at her watch. I was so tempted to invite Jackson over, but I knew that, if I did, my last hope for getting another shot at the popcorn would disappear.

"No, it's getting late," I said, folding like a bad flan. "And we'll be going to bed soon."

"Okay," Jackson said. "I'll just leave you a message. Goodnight."

I tossed my phone on the coffee table and rubbed the sleeping Chloe's head.

"Well done," Chef Claire said, returning the two bowls of popcorn to their rightful owners."

"So, what's the deal with Freddie and Jackson?" Josie said.

"What do you mean?" Chef Claire said.

"Are you eventually going to agree to date either one of them?" Josie said, reaching for her wine glass.

"Who says I haven't already agreed?" Chef Claire said, grinning at us.

"Really?" Josie said, glancing at me. "Which one?"

"Why both of them, of course," Chef Claire said.

"What?" Josie said.

"And you never said a word to us?" I said, going for mock indignation, but sounding a bit too shrill to my own ears.

"I swore myself to secrecy," Chef Claire said. "And you can't say a word. They don't know."

"You little devil," Josie said, laughing.

"So, you've got your own version of catch and release going on," I said.

"No, that's the problem," Chef Claire said, turning serious. "Actually, I'm afraid I might be dealing with two potential keepers. I like them both. A lot."

"Wow. Now that's a surprise," I said. "Is there anything we can do?"

"Yeah," Chef Claire said, staring at TV. "Pass the popcorn."

Chapter 7

I was eating breakfast with Josie and Chef Claire when I finally remembered to check my phone messages. I thought about listening to it right away but remembered that my detective skills always worked better on a full stomach.

In the interest of full disclosure for those of you wondering: whole wheat walnut pancakes, apple butter syrup, bacon, and apple slices sauteed in nutmeg and cinnamon. Final score on the pancakes: Josie 4; Suzy 3. But I did manage to hold my own on the bacon front.

I cleared the breakfast dishes and stacked the dishwasher then sat back down at the table and listened to Jackson's message. I jotted down the information and slid my phone into my pocket.

"It's a corporate account," I said. "A company based in Albany."

"Jerome probably worked there," Josie said.

"Or he used to work there before he ended up in jail," I said, refilling our coffee mugs.

"Or maybe he was hired after he made parole," Josie said. "Maybe he was in some program that tries to rehabilitate criminals."

"I doubt it," I said. "Jackson said last night that the Albany cops lost track of Jerome soon after he got released. And if he'd been around here all that time, could he still have been employed by them?"

"What's the name of the company?" Josie said.

I checked my hen-scratched note.

"I think it says Fullerbome Security," I said, squinting at the piece of paper. "No, check that. It's Fullerton Security."

Josie shook her head at me.

"What can I say? I have a hard time listening and writing at the same time," I said, shrugging.

"Should we just give them a call?" Josie said.

"No, it would be too easy for them to lie to us over the phone," I said. "I want to see the reaction we get when we start asking questions."

"Why do you assume that they are going to lie to us?" Josie said.

"I'm not assuming anything," I said. "I'm just trying to minimize the chance they could get away with it if they try."

"You want to drive to Albany?" Josie said.

"Sure. Why not? We can be there in about three hours. Everything is fine down at the Inn, you don't have any surgeries scheduled, and it's a beautiful day for a road trip."

"They're predicting a snowstorm for later on," she said.

"What do they know?"

Josie shook her head at me again and checked her schedule on her phone.

"This morning I've got three annual checkups. After that, I'm clear. But I have to tell you, this looks like another one of your wild goose chases, Suzy."

"Maybe."

We were on the road by noon, armed with a fully loaded picnic basket courtesy of Chef Claire. Ten minutes into the trip, we hit 81 South and Josie poured two cups of tomato basil soup from a thermos. A half hour later, she removed two roast beef sandwiches that included a horseradish-dill mayo that almost caused me to drive off the road when I tasted it. By the time we hit 90 East that would take us to Albany, we were well into the chocolate fudge brownies and making a real mess of the inside of my SUV.

I glanced over at Josie whose face was smeared with chocolate.

"Take human bites," I said, laughing.

43

"Don't blame me," she said. "It's your driving."

I handed her a napkin, then another.

We exited the Thruway and located Fullerton Security on the west side of the city. We pulled into a small parking lot in front of a modest two-story brick building and walked inside. A receptionist greeted us and remained friendly even after she learned that we didn't have an appointment but still wanted to meet with the owner. Two minutes later, a tall, middle-aged man stepped into the reception area and greeted us. We waited out his inevitable lingering gaze at Josie, then shook hands.

"It's nice to meet you, ladies," Tom Fullerton said, pleasantly. "Let's go to my office. Would you like coffee? Maybe a snack?"

"I could eat," Josie said.

He gestured for us to continue to his office while he stopped to chat with the receptionist. As we walked, I caught Josie's eye, and she shrugged.

"Interrogation always makes me hungry," she said.

Fullerton entered, closed the door, and gestured at two chairs in front of his desk. We sat down and looked around. The only thing I learned from all the photos on his wall was that the man seemed to love the woman in the photos and golf. The two of them were grinning wildly on at least two dozen different courses around the world. He noticed my interest and glanced around the display.

"That's me and my ex-wife, Georgia, at Pebble Beach," he said, smiling and pointing at one of the photos.

"It's a beautiful area," I said.

"I shot 75 that day," he said.

All I knew about golf was that the smaller the number, the better. So I decided to go for it and rolled the dice.

"That's a great score," I said.

"Thanks," he said, his smile widening.

"Good guess," Josie whispered.

I punched her in the leg but kept smiling up at the photo.

"Sorry to hear about your marriage," I said.

"Yeah, thanks," he whispered. "Things happen, right? She still has a small piece of the company so it can be a bit awkward when we're forced to see each other. But we're getting better at being cordial."

"I understand," I said. "That must be hard."

"I'm still holding out hope for reconciliation at some point," he whispered.

It sounded like he was trying to convince himself more than us, so Josie and I merely nodded our support.

"So what brings you two all the way from Clay Bay completely unannounced on a cold day like this?"

I briefly explained who Josie and I were and what we did for a living, then launched into a short overview of the puppy mill we'd discovered. He leaned back in his chair and frowned.

"They were doing that to dogs?" he said, scowling.

"Yes," I said.

"And now you're trying to find out who they are?"

"Yes," Josie said.

"I can certainly understand that. It's a despicable thing to do to defenseless animals," he said. "But why on earth are you here?"

"We're trying to find out some information about somebody we think used to work for you," I said.

"Used to work here?" he said, his eyes narrowing.

"Yes. A gentleman, and I'm using that term very loosely, by the name of Jerome Jefferson," I said.

He shook his head and exhaled loudly.

"Oh, no," he said. "Jerome. Don't tell me Jerome is mixed up in this thing."

"No, actually, Jerome isn't mixed up in anything at the moment," Josie said. "He's dead."

"What?" Fullerton said, stunned by the news. "But how? What happened to him?"

"He was shot," I said.

"Where?"

"Right in the middle of the forehead," Josie said.

It wasn't one of Josie's subtler moments, but at least it was better than telling him Jerome had caught one in the brainpan.

"Actually," Fullerton said, "I was referring to the actual location of where he was shot."

"Oh. I'm sorry about that," Josie said. "He was shot in a small town outside of Clay Bay."

"Was it some sort of altercation in a bar?"

"No, he was in a phone booth making a call," I said.

"A phone booth?" he said, thoroughly confused. "Who uses a phone booth these days?"

"Our guess is that he didn't want any trace of the call showing up on cell phone history," I said.

"I guess that makes sense," Fullerton said. "Given Jerome's fondness for all things nefarious, I can see why he might want to do that. Who was he calling?"

I glanced at Josie, and she gave me the slightest shake of her head.

"We don't know. It appears Jerome may not have had time to make the call," Josie said.

The door opened, and the receptionist entered with coffee and a stack of chocolate chip cookies. We fixed our coffee, grabbed two cookies each, and sat quietly for a few minutes. Fullerton appeared to be completely shocked by the news.

"We'd lost touch with Jerome recently," Fullerton said.

"So he did work here?" I said.

Fullerton laughed and shook his head sadly.

"Yes, he did. For about a month after his last release from prison," he said. "Georgia made me hire him."

"Your ex-wife?" I said, glancing at Josie and nodding at the cookies.

They were very good.

"Jerome was Georgia's brother," Fullerton said. "They'd been estranged for years, but then their folks passed on, and she decided that some form of reconciliation was required."

"Sure, sure," Josie said, munching on a cookie. "Family, right?"

"Exactly," Fullerton said. "So I agreed to take him on. Big mistake on my part."

"What does your company do, Mr. Fullerton?" I said.

"Home and corporate security systems," he said, then let loose with a snort that sounded like he was going for ironic.

"You hired a guy with multiple convictions for breaking and entering and armed robbery to work for your security company?" I said.

"Yeah, it wasn't one of my finest moments," he said. "But Georgia can be very persuasive when she wants to be. And she wouldn't let it go."

"Does your ex-wife work here as well?" I said.

"No, Georgia's a brilliant technologist and a consultant for many of the companies in Tech Valley."

I'd heard of Tech Valley in the past and knew that it was a loosely-defined area that ran about 250 miles from New York City all the way to the Canadian border and included many companies that dealt with a variety of technologies and sciences I know absolutely nothing about.

"And I'm sure you're very familiar with all the important work many of the Tech Valley companies are doing," he said.

"Of course, of course," I said, rubbing my chin.

"Smooth," Josie whispered.

I punched her leg again as I continued to rub my chin sagely.

Just call me Bodhisattva.

"So what happened after you agreed to hire Jerome?" I said.

"Quite a lot actually," he said, again shaking his head. "And all of it bad."

"Interesting," I said.

"Not really," he said. "But as I've reminded Georgia several times, it was certainly predictable."

"Let me guess, he started robbing the houses where you'd installed security systems?" I said.

"Worse. Jerome started selling the access codes to other criminals. We had a rash of robberies in the area and we soon realized that they were all customers of ours. Of course, the first thing that popped into my head was that Jerome was conducting the robberies, but he always had an airtight alibi. Then I finally figured out what he was doing, and Georgia and I confronted him. I fired him on the spot, threatened to call the police, and he simply disappeared. Today is the first bit of news I've heard about him since then."

"We're sorry we have such bad news for you," I said.

He shrugged and suddenly seemed to shrink in his chair.

"What a waste of a life," he said. "I can't believe he and my ex-wife came out of the same gene pool. She's so intelligent and accomplished. Jerome was a total screw up."

Josie nudged me with her foot. I got the message.

"Let me ask you one more question, Mr. Fullerton," I said.

"Sure. Go ahead."

"Did Jerome have a company-assigned cell phone when he worked for you?"

"Yes, we give them to all our employees. It's a nice little benefit for them, and it helps us keep a relatively close eye on our folks," he said, noticing our reaction to his last comment. "As I've learned over the years, when it comes to running a security company, you can never be too careful when it comes to the people who are working for you."

"And that was something Jerome reconfirmed for you," Josie said.

"Yes. He certainly did," Fullerton said.

"Do you remember if you got his phone back when you fired him?" I said.

He thought about it for several moments as if replaying a scene in his head.

"No, I don't think we did. After I had fired him, he stormed out of the office, and that's the last time I saw Jerome. But the phone number would have been disconnected."

"It was disconnected," I said. "Yesterday. The day after he was killed."

"What?" Fullerton said, his eyes wide. "But he's been gone for months."

"We thought it was a bit strange," I said.

"It certainly is," he said. "And it's something I will definitely be looking into."

"Would it be too much to ask for you to give us a call when you figure it out? Josie and I take puppy mills very personally."

"No, I'll be happy to do that," he said. "But it makes no sense. Jerome seemed to detest most of the people he came in contact with, but he absolutely loved dogs."

I slid one of our business cards across the desk. Fullerton stared down at it, then looked up.

"I'm sorry, ladies, but if you will excuse me, I have a very difficult phone call to make. Georgia is going to be devastated."

We stood, shook hands with him, and left him sitting at his desk. On our way out we thanked the receptionist who gave us four more cookies for the road. We climbed in the SUV and by the time we hit Route 90 West, the snow had started and was already beginning to accumulate.

"What do you think?" I said.

"About Fullerton?" Josie said, finishing the last cookie.

"Yeah."

"He was genuinely shocked, or he's one of the best actors I've ever seen," Josie said.

"I agree. Did you buy his my ex-wife made me do it bit about why he hired Jerome?"

"I did," Josie said, keeping a close eye on the emerging snowstorm. "Why else would he hire a guy with that history? Fullerton had a lot to lose and nothing to gain except getting her off his back."

"If mama ain't happy, ain't nobody happy," I said, laughing.

"Exactly."

Chapter 8

"Could you please change the channel?"

"I thought you'd never ask," Josie said, reaching for the radio buttons. "I'm so burned out on Christmas carols."

"That's because all the stores started playing them before Halloween."

I squeezed the steering wheel hard and tried turning my windshield wipers on again. The only thing the wipers did was make my visibility worse, so I turned them off. The refrain of Walking in a Winter Wonderland disappeared and was replaced by smooth jazz. People may wax poetic about walking in a winter wonderland, and it has its moments, but driving in one was another story altogether. At least a foot of snow had fallen since we'd left Albany and it looked like our three-hour drive home might double. Fortunately, the plows were out and doing a good job keeping the Thruway and Route 81 driveable. North of Syracuse, there was a stretch where the snow was particularly heavy, and we fell in behind a snowplow and followed it for the next twenty miles. By the time the plow exited the highway, the snowfall had slowed, and we headed for home at a constant speed of forty-five on the snow-covered, but relatively safe, road.

We arrived home just before midnight to the sight of a freshly plowed driveway and shoveled sidewalks. All the lights were on at the Inn and, at first, Josie and I were concerned that something had happened. But we relaxed when we saw Jackson and Sammy smiling and waving their gloved hands at us. I pulled into the driveway, and we both headed straight for the Inn. Jackson met us on the porch.

"What do you think?" Jackson said, gesturing at the driveway.

"It's great," I said. "Who did the plowing?"

"I did," he said, pointing at his truck that had a snowplow attached off the front. "It's my new toy. I've been driving around all night testing it out."

"You're hired," Josie said, laughing.

"Who shoveled all the paths and sidewalk?" I said.

"Sammy," Jackson said.

"We so need to give him a raise," Josie said, glancing around and nodding her head in approval.

We headed inside to check on the dogs. Sammy greeted us with two steaming mugs of hot chocolate.

"Thanks, Sammy," I said, accepting one of the mugs.

The kid was really on his game tonight.

"And great job with the shoveling. You didn't have to do that. We have a couple of high school kids we pay to do it."

"No problem, Suzy," Sammy said with a huge grin plastered on his face. "I figured that since I was already here working, what the heck. Hey, Josie."

"Hi, Sammy," she said, nodding at his goofy grin. "Call me crazy, but nobody should be that happy after doing all that shoveling."

"No, it's not that. C'mon, follow me. I've got something to show you."

We followed him into the back and stopped in front of the condo where the six Cocker Spaniel puppies were housed. Jill was sitting on the floor feeding two of them with baby bottles of milk. She did her best to wave hello and refocused on the puppies.

"What did you want to show us?" I said, suddenly feeling very tired.

"Watch," Sammy said. He whistled softly. "Tripod. Come here, boy."

From the group of four Cockers that were sleeping on a plush dog bed, one of the puppies lifted its head and then stood and wobbled toward Sammy's voice on three legs. Josie and I both started bawling on the spot. I wiped the tears away with the back of my hand and watched as the puppy made its way into Sammy's arms.

"He's walking," Josie said.

"He sure is," Sammy said, still beaming. "About two hours ago. He's still trying to figure everything out, but that's a good sign, right?"

"It certainly is," Josie said, stroking one of Tripod's ears.

"How's the rest of the litter doing, Jill?" I said when I'd regained my composure.

"You tell me," she said, laughing.

She gently rolled the two puppies she was feeding over on their backs, and we couldn't help chuckling at their chubby tummies as they kicked their little legs in the air.

"I weighed them all earlier, and they're still a couple pounds lighter than normal, but I'm betting they'll catch up sometime next week. They're all eating like a horse."

"Good. Keep fattening them up. How are the lab puppies doing?" Josie said.

"They're great," Jill said. "And we had two more of them adopted this afternoon. That makes eight."

"They should be ready to go by the 24th. There's going to be some very happy kids on Christmas morning," Josie said.

Jackson poked his head inside the condo area.

"Got a minute?" he said.

We said our goodbyes to the dogs and Sammy and Jill and gestured for Jackson to follow us up the shoveled path that led to the house. Chloe and Chef Claire greeted us at the door, and we sat down in the living room. I couldn't help but notice some tension between Chef Claire and Jackson. But I was too tired to dwell on it. Chef Claire excused herself and went to bed. Chloe climbed up on my lap and promptly fell asleep.

"How did it go today?" Jackson said, yawning.

We gave him an update on our meeting with Fullerton and answered Jackson's questions the best we could.

"I guess it makes sense that the owner of a company wouldn't necessarily know that a cell number hadn't been disconnected," Jackson said. "But it still seems odd since the guy was his brother in law, not to mention a career criminal."

"He said he'd call when he figured out how it happened," I said.

"Do you see any connection between him and the murder or the puppy mill?" he said.

Josie and I both shook our heads.

"Are you having any luck with the murder?" I said.

"Not really. But I did talk to somebody who'd been drinking all day at the Outer Limit, and he thinks he might have seen Jerome there with two other guys earlier that evening."

"I guess that's something to go on," Josie said.

"This guy has also been known to see pink elephants and alien spacecraft in his driveway," Jackson said.

"Ah, got it," Josie said, laughing.

"We've got nothing," Jackson said. "And if Jerome hadn't been able to make the call to you guys before getting shot, the way that phone booth is tucked away behind that vacant building, he could have ended up spending the whole winter there with nobody noticing."

"Now there's a pleasant thought," Josie said, scrunching up her face. "Geez, Jackson. Really?"

"What?" Jackson said, staring at Josie. "It's true."

"I'm trying to get into the Christmas spirit here," Josie said. "Now I'm probably going to have nightmares."

"Well, excuse me for pointing out a simple fact," Jackson said.

"Guys, please. It's too late for this," I said. "But he did make the call. And that was after he dropped the litter of Cockers off on our doorstep. Fullerton mentioned that Jerome was a dog lover."

"So what was Jerome trying to do? Bust up a puppy mill?" Jackson said. "Is that enough of a reason to get shot?"

"It would be for me," I said. "Not to shoot Jerome who was apparently trying to shut it down. But I'd certainly think about doing it to the people operating the mill."

"Me too," Josie said.

"Thanks for the warning," Jackson said, laughing. "But I'm not buying it. It feels light for a motive. There has to be more to it than that."

"Like what?" Josie said.

"I don't know," Jackson said.

"Maybe they were using the dogs as cover for something else," I said.

Josie and Jackson nodded and thought about my comment.

Even in the dark of night, my ability to identify possible solutions to problems was, in my humble opinion, unparalleled.

Then they both shrugged simultaneously.

"Like what?" Jackson said.

"Smuggling?" I eventually managed to mumble.

Okay, maybe unparalleled was a bit of an overreach. But in my defense, it was late.

"What could you smuggle in a puppy?" Josie said.

"Not much," I conceded.

What a total whiff on my part. It was definitely time to go to bed.

We sat in silence for several minutes before Jackson stood and pulled on his coat.

"Look, it's late," he said. "Why don't we continue this conversation over breakfast? There's something else I'd like to talk to you about. I'll even buy."

I glanced at Josie who nodded.

"We're in. The Café around nine work for you?" I said.

"Perfect. See you then," he said, heading for the door.

"What else do you think he wants to talk to us about?" Josie said, standing up to stretch as she yawned.

"I'm sure it's about me."

We both turned and saw Chef Claire standing in her robe.

"Did something happen between you two?" I said.

"Kind of," Chef Claire said. "Jackson and Freddie had a fight this afternoon. They almost came to blows."

"What?" Josie said.

"Yeah, it got ugly in a hurry."

"They were fighting over you?"

"No, they were fighting over which of them had the right to go out with me," Chef Claire said, shaking her head in disgust.

"I knew those two geniuses would figure out a way to screw things up," Josie said.

"I was standing right there, and it was as if I was invisible," Chef Claire said. "It was like I didn't have any say in who I was, or wasn't going to, date."

"They know better than that," I said.

"Obviously not," Josie said.

"We're having breakfast with Jackson," I said. "We'll have a word with him."

"Yes, I heard. But it doesn't matter," Chef Claire said. "Excuse the bad metaphor, but for the time being I've put both of them on the back burner."

"You should have stuck their heads in the oven," Josie said. "What a couple of Neanderthals. And all this time I thought both of them at least knew how to walk upright."

"I'm sorry about this, Chef Claire," I said.

"Yeah, I'm not very happy about it myself."

"You know," Josie said. "I've always found that a little snack helps me work my way through problems like this."

Chef Claire laughed. I shook my head at Josie but had to admit that raiding the fridge sounded like a good idea.

"We've got a bunch of that chicken chili left from the other night," Chef Claire said.

"Perfect," I said.

"I could eat."

Chapter 9

After we had each devoured a plate of home fries, two English muffins and a Western omelet the size of a Frisbee, Josie and I started working on Jackson. By the time we were finished, he was huddled in the corner on his side of the booth and picking at his breakfast. When he finally quit offering lame excuses for his behavior and promised to apologize profusely to Chef Claire, we relented and focused on our hot chocolate.

Jackson glanced up when he heard the Café door open. He scowled when he saw the two men.

"Great," he said. "I wonder who the genius was that decided to let those two out."

"Who is it?" Josie said, turning around for a look.

I turned around, recognized the men, then shook my head.

"What?" Josie said, glancing back and forth at our reactions.

"It's the Baxter Brothers," Jackson said. "Billy and Bobby."

"Now those are two ugly human beings," Josie said, sneaking another peek. "Which one's which?"

"It doesn't matter," I said. "There's not a bit of difference."

"I think Billy might be piled a bit higher," Jackson said, laughing.

"I've never seen them before," Josie said. "Are they locals?"

"Yeah," I said. "When they aren't in jail." I looked at Jackson. "I thought they got five years."

"They did," Jackson said.

"It couldn't have been five years already," I said.

"Do you think the Baxter Brothers got out early for good behavior, Suzy?" Jackson said.

"You've got a point there," I said, frowning. "Wow. That was five years ago?"

"They got five years for doing what?" Josie said.

"They broke into an eighty-year-old woman's house, robbed her, and then beat her up," Jackson said.

"And they only got five years?" Josie said.

"Yeah," I said.

"That's unbelievable," Josie said.

"Welcome to my world," Jackson said. "Those two are a couple of beauties. They come from a long line of River smugglers. Their grandfather was a legendary bootlegger around the area during Prohibition."

"And after Prohibition ended, he moved into smuggling people back and forth across the border," I said. "Apparently he used to laugh that if he'd known how much money he could make smuggling in Chinese workers, he never would have even bothered with bootlegging."

"Lovely," Josie said. "And we thought that the people operating that puppy mill were the despicable ones."

I stared at Josie, then looked across the table at Jackson. He'd picked up on Josie's offhand comment as well.

"Wow, now there's a thought," Jackson said.

The Baxter Brothers approached our table and stood staring down at us. They both nodded at Jackson and me and then fixed their creepy leer on Josie. Josie maintained eye contact, and eventually both brothers looked away.

"Hey, Chief," the brother named Billy said.

"Hi, Billy. Bobby. When did you two get out?" Jackson said.

"About six months ago," Bobby said.

"Really? How about that? And you're still out walking the street," Jackson said.

"You always were pretty funny for a small town cop, Chief."

"So what have you two been up to?" Jackson said.

"Oh, a little of this, a little of that," Bobby said. "Mostly traveling. You know, catching up with friends."

"Well, that should have got you through Monday morning," I said. "What did you do the rest of the six months?"

Josie snorted.

"Ah, little Suzy Chandler," Billy said. "Such a pretty woman who spends all her time on dogs."

"Yeah, and we're pretty busy at the moment. We just added a whole bunch of dogs to the family."

He eyes narrowed for a second, then he recovered.

"Well, you always did consider yourself a bit of a saint," Bobby said.

"I have my moments."

"Are you two staying in town?" Jackson said. "I haven't seen you around."

"No, we got a place out of town," Billy said. "But we'll be around for the holidays, so you'll probably be seeing us."

"I can't wait," Jackson said.

The Baxter Brother named Bobby resumed leering at Josie.

"And what are you asking Santa for this year, cutie pie?"

"I'm still trying to decide," Josie said. "But if this conversation continues much longer, probably a rabies shot."

"Oh, would you look at that, Bobby. We got a feisty one here." A grin of unadulterated evil appeared on his face as he looked back at Josie. "I like feisty."

"Like it?" Josie said. "You can't even spell it."

He glared at Josie and then turned to his brother.

"Let's go, Billy. Never let it be said that the Baxter Brothers hang around places where they aren't wanted."

"So why are you still in town?" I said.

Josie snorted again.

"Watch yourself, girlie," Billy said, glaring down at me. "I don't appreciate it when a woman tries to make a fool out of me."

"I can understand that," I said. "You've always struck me as a do-it-yourself kind of guy."

"Oh, good one," Josie whispered.

"I don't like rude women either," Billy said.

"Go away," Jackson said.

The Baxter Brothers stared back at him, then nodded.

"Sure, Chief. Whatever you say," Billy said. "Hope to see you folks around, but if we don't cross paths, have a Merry Christmas."

"Catch you later," Jackson said.

"In your dreams," Billy said, laughing as they headed for a booth in the back of the diner.

Jackson paid our bill, and we left.

On the way back to the Inn, Josie and I discussed the Baxter Brothers in less than glowing terms. Although we did decide that we were definitely going to have to come up with a plan to see them again shortly.

We were still going back and forth about the need for a preemptive rabies shot.

Chapter 10

We had initially believed that spotting and following the Baxter Brothers in and around a small town like Clay Bay would be a slam dunk. On a side note, I was doing my best to avoid using the term piece of cake around Josie since every time I did, Josie reacted like a Pavlovian dog trained to respond to a bell and added a stop at Paterson's bakery to our itinerary. But locating the infamous pair for the purpose of tracking their movements had proven harder than either of us had believed possible.

For the past three evenings, we had driven past every bar, club, and restaurant we could think of within a thirty-mile radius hoping to spot their truck but had come up empty. We didn't even know if following the Baxter Brothers around would help us identify the operators of the puppy mill and who had killed Jerome Jefferson, but it was all we had.

"I think I need help," I said as I stretched out on the couch and realized my jeans were fighting back. "Nobody should eat that much food. I can barely fit into these pants."

"You just washed them, right?" Josie said, easing herself into one of the overstuffed chairs in front of the fireplace.

"Yeah, but what does that have to do with my eating everything within reach?" I said.

"The jeans probably just shrunk in the dryer. They'll stretch out," she said.

"Not as much as my stomach is stretching. But maybe you're right," I said, feeling a bit better about what I knew was starting to become a problem.

I'd gained another three pounds since Thanksgiving and while my table manners had marginally improved, the changes I'd made at the table to appear more ladylike, as my mother insists on calling it, hadn't made a dent in my overall consumption.

"We'll deal with it after the holidays," Josie said. "No sane person starts a diet this time of year."

I wasn't even going to try arguing with rock-solid logic like that.

"We must be doing something wrong," I said, moving off the dreaded weight gain topic.

"Yeah, those two cretins can't be that hard to find," Josie said. "And they're definitely not the stay at home type. What are we missing?"

"Maybe all their criminal buddies are throwing Christmas parties, and that's keeping them out of the bars," I said.

"Geez, can you imagine that?" Josie said, laughing. "A keg, tequila shooters, and a little game of B&E Yankee Swap."

"Don't make me laugh," I said, holding my stomach. "I'm too full."

"So if the Baxter Brothers aren't out celebrating the holidays, what are they doing?"

"Probably working," I said.

Wow. Where did that come from? Thank you, Ms. Subconscious.

I sat up on the couch, waking Chloe in the process. She gave me the evil eye and removed herself from my lap and found going solo on the remaining two-thirds of the couch more to her liking.

"And if they're working, they're out committing crimes," I said. "But Jackson said yesterday that things are very quiet at the moment."

"Maybe the Baxter boys are robbing the houses of people who are away for the holidays," Josie said. "Maybe nobody has noticed yet."

"Could be," I said. "But I have a feeling that those two have moved onto something bigger and more lucrative than simple burglary."

"Well, they do come from a family of smugglers," Josie said.

"Yeah," I said.

Then I had an idea and picked up my phone. I dialed Jackson and put the phone on speaker.

"This is Jackson."

"Hey, it's me."

"Hi, Suzy," Jackson said. "What's up?"

"We were just sitting here talking," I said.

"I really wish you two would stop doing that," Jackson said, sounding out of sorts.

"Funny," I said. "What prison did the Baxter Brothers just come out of?"

"They were in Adirondack Correctional, a medium-security joint near Lake Placid," Jackson said.

"How about Jerome?" I said.

"You know, since he was dead, I didn't even bother to check," Jackson said. "Hang on. I'm sure I've got it here somewhere."

We heard the sound of papers being shuffled around interspersed with Jackson's mild cursing. Then he came back on the line.

"Bingo. Jerome was at Adirondack the same time as the Baxter Brothers."

"Interesting," I said.

"Yes, it certainly is," Jackson said. "I should have connected the dots on that one."

"Well," I said, grinning at Josie. "You've had a lot on your mind lately."

"Don't start," Jackson said.

"How did your apology tour go?"

64

"You know exactly how it went," Jackson said. "Now is there anything else you need from me or can I get back to feeling sorry for myself?"

"Just one more thing," I said. "Have there been any crimes reported lately?"

"You mean since you asked me yesterday?"

"Yes."

"No. Can I go now?"

"Sure. Have a good evening, Jackson."

"Whatever."

"Well, ho-ho-ho to you, too."

I ended the call and got up to toss another log on the fire. It flared and woke Chloe. Deciding a nap in front of the fireplace sounded like a good idea, she hopped off the couch and stretched out in front of the fire.

"So now we know that the Baxter Brothers knew Jerome," I said.

"And Jerome came here after he got fired by Fullerton Security," Josie said. "It couldn't have just been a coincidence."

"Not a chance," I said, starting to feel a bit better as my digestive system started working overtime on my dinner.

"So what do we do with that bit of information?" Josie said.

"Well, it basically confirms that the three of them were working together. And since Jerome was the one who rescued the Cocker puppies, we know he had a problem with whatever scam they were working," I said.

"Or maybe Jerome only had a problem with part of the plan," Josie said.

"The part that dealt with the puppy mill?"

"Yeah," she said.

"But if the puppy mill wasn't their primary focus, why would they even bother with it?"

"I don't know," Josie said. "A lucrative sideline, maybe. They wouldn't get rich selling black market dogs, but they could make some decent money. Especially if they moved a lot of dogs."

"But to move that many, they would have to use pet stores, right?" I said.

"Yeah, primarily. They couldn't make enough money selling to individual families," Josie said.

"Since most puppy mills sell across state lines, the delivery logistics alone would have been a nightmare," I said.

"Yeah, I don't see the individual family approach happening. They would have to be working with a network of pet stores. But Jackson said that the state police checked out all the pet businesses in the region and didn't come up with anything remotely suspicious," Josie said.

"Hmmm," I said.

"What?"

"I was just thinking that maybe we've been looking on the wrong side of the River," I said.

"But the Baxter Brothers are convicted felons. The second they showed up at Canadian Immigration, they'd be red flagged. Especially if they were driving a van full of puppies, right?"

"Sure. If they were driving a car. You've lived here long enough to know that a boat is a different story altogether," I said.

"A boat? This time of year?"

"Can you think of a better time?" I said.

"Absolutely," Josie said, laughing. "Any other time of year."

"For them," I said, laughing along. "Not us. It's perfect. Nobody would be crazy enough to be out on the River right now."

"Except maybe the Baxter Brothers?"

"Yes. And that's probably what they're thinking. It's absolutely freezing out there on the River, but there's no real ice yet. At least not enough that would do any real damage to a boat, especially one that's been built to deal with something like that."

"Didn't they say at the diner that they would be around through the holidays and then taking some time off?" Josie said.

"They did," I said, nodding. "And that would be right around the time the shoreline freezes solid."

"It sounds like an awful lot of trouble to go through. I mean we're talking about puppies."

"I think you were right earlier when you mentioned that the puppies might just be a sideline. To a smuggler, a couple litters of puppies would just be more one thing to deliver. To them, they're not pets, they're contraband."

"And when Jerome found out about the puppy mill, he tried to do something to stop it," Josie said. "You think the Baxter's are the ones who shot him?"

"I'm not sure," I said. "But for now, let's call it a working theory."

"Well, if your working theory turns out to be correct, the Baxter boys wouldn't think twice about shooting us," Josie said.

"They are delightful creatures, aren't they?" I said, grinning at her.

"I'm so glad you're taking this seriously," Josie said, shaking her head.

"Relax," I said. "We'll never find ourselves in a position to get shot."

"You mean a position like bound and gagged with a pistol pointed at the back of our head?"

"You worry too much," I said.

"Yeah, I'm the problem here," Josie said, getting up to stoke the fire. "But we're still stuck with the question of how to find them."

"We've been coming at it all wrong," I said. "If we consider the possibility that the Baxter Brothers are using a boat, there's only one place they could be operating out of at this time of year."

"You lost me," Josie said.

"You feel like taking a drive?" I said, getting up off the couch.

"Not really," Josie said.

"Come on. It'll be fun."

"Gee, Suzy. Why don't I believe you?"

Chapter 11

Rooster Jennings was a local legend and one of my favorite people. For those who eventually came to understand and appreciate the man and why he did the things he did, Rooster was an acquired taste. And for everyone else who crossed paths with him, Rooster Jennings was a man who left a very bad taste in your mouth and was someone to be avoided at all costs.

He'd grown up in the area, and apart from the year and a half he'd spent in Vietnam before being honorably discharged from the Army who, rumor had it, was more than happy to get rid of him, Rooster had, literally, never spent a night outside of Clay Bay. Except once for a Grateful Dead show in Ottawa in the early 80's he still waxed on about philosophically.

He'd returned from Vietnam with a fondness for weed, a deep mistrust of all corporate and government entities, and a commitment to black-market economies. Rooster had inherited a small stretch of shoreline on the outskirts of town from his grandparents and ran an operation that ostensibly consisted of a small engine repair business, boat storage, and a single gas pump on his dock he activated during the summer where he charged exorbitant prices to unsuspecting tourists.

Rooster hunted out of season, fished whenever and wherever the heck he wanted to and thumbed his nose at all forms of regulatory bodies and those who worked for them on both sides of the River. Over time, those officials, and pretty much everybody else, adopted a hands-off policy when it came to Rooster. And that was just the way he liked it.

But Rooster loved dogs and we had hit if off since we'd met when I was still a young girl.

We found him tinkering with an old outboard motor under a single lightbulb dangling from the ceiling in his makeshift workspace near his docks. Despite the time of year, there were still several boats in the water, and I heard the gurgling of the aeration machines used to keep ice from forming on the sides of the boats at night. He glanced up when he heard our approach and grinned at me.

"Well, I'll be. Suzy Chandler," Rooster said, wiping his greasy hands with an even greasier rag. "What the heck brings you down here on a cold night like this?"

Despite the cold, he was only wearing a ZZ Top tee shirt under an unbuttoned flannel shirt. His jeans, held up by an American flag set of suspenders, were tucked into a pair of old workboats without laces. His long greasy, gray hair was tied back in a ponytail that trailed down his back. He grinned at me and spat a mouthful of tobacco in the general direction of my foot. Josie took a step back.

"Let me guess," Josie whispered. "He's the Baxter Brothers' long lost cousin."

"Relax. The tobacco spit is a sign of affection," I whispered.

"I'd hate to see what happens when he gets turned on," she whispered.

"Hi, Rooster. It's good to see you," I said.

"Been too long," he said.

Then he got his first look at Josie. He blinked several times, then shook his head.

"My word," Rooster said. "I thought the sunrise this morning was about the most beautiful thing the man upstairs could pull off. I was wrong."

I laughed. Josie was still searching for her sense of humor.

"Rooster, I'd like you to meet my best friend and business partner, Josie."

"So you're the vet I've heard so much about," Rooster said, unable to take his eyes off her. "You be sure and let me know if you ever start working on people."

I laughed again. This time Josie managed a small chuckle.

"Say, I've been thinking about gettin' another dog," Rooster said. "You got any at the moment?"

"We've got tons," I said. "What are you looking for?"

"Something big, loyal, and able to scare the crap out of tourists when necessary."

This time both Josie and I laughed.

"We've got a male pit bull, but he's getting up there in years."

"No, I need a young one. I've had a couple of older rescues in the past, but it's too hard saying goodbye to them," Rooster said, wiping away a tear and a painful memory.

"In a couple of weeks, we're going to have some labs ready for adoption. And in a couple of months, we're expecting a litter of German Shepherds."

"That's the one," Rooster said. "A big male German Shepherd. You put me on the list and let me know when I should swing by."

"You got it, Rooster."

"So how can I help you?"

"Actually, we're here because of the dogs," I said.

I spent a few minutes explaining the puppy mill. Apparently, this was the first time Rooster had heard the news, and he wasn't pleased with it.

"People," he said, shaking his head.

"Yeah, we know," I said. "We're trying to track a couple of people we think could be involved."

"Who's that?"

"The Baxter Brothers," I said.

71

"Those two," Rooster said. "Why aren't I surprised?"

"Have you seen them?"

"Sure. They rented some dock space from me."

"When was that?"

"Probably two, no three months ago," he said.

"Odd that they'd be renting dock space at the end of the summer wouldn't you say?" I said.

"Suzy, we've known each other a long time, right?"

"Yes, Rooster. A long time," I said, knowing what was coming next.

"I'm just a poor businessman trying to get by. What my customers do is none of my business. And that's the reason why I have so many repeat customers. The Baxter boys are pure scum, but as long as they pay me a hundred bucks by the first of each month, my interest in how they spend their time is pretty much zilch."

"Unless you knew they were messing with dogs, right?" I said.

"Yeah," he said nodding. "If that's the case, then my level of interest would definitely go up. How sure are you that they're involved?"

"At the moment, I'd probably go as high as ninety percent," I said.

"Okay," he said, thinking for several seconds before continuing. "They usually take their boat out a couple nights a week. Tuesday and Thursday nights around ten if memory serves. And they're usually back by midnight, one at the latest. Their boat is the black runabout in the third slip to my left. I wouldn't have a clue where they go."

"Thanks, Rooster," I said, hugging him. "Don't worry, we won't tell anybody where we got our information."

"I know you won't," he said. "That's why I told you."

"We'll let you know as soon as the litter arrives," I said, waving goodbye as we headed back to the car.

"Hey, Suzy," Rooster called after us.

"Yeah."

"If you need any help with the Baxter boys, let me know. I've got some friends who'd be more than happy to help them adjust their attitude about dogs."

"I'll keep that in mind, Rooster. Thanks."

I started the car and cranked up the heater.

"Tee shirt and flannel shirt with no socks," Josie said. "Why isn't he in the hospital with pneumonia?"

"He comes from hardy stock," I said, shrugging. "And I'm sure the bottle of Remy Martin helps him fend off the cold."

"Remy Martin? That stuff can go for a couple of hundred a bottle."

"Rooster's loaded," I said.

"After a bottle of Remy a night, I'm sure he is."

"No, I meant loaded as in rich," I said, laughing.

"That guy?"

"Rumor has it that he's worth millions," I said.

"No way."

"Yeah, at least that's the story."

"How?" Josie said.

"I have no idea," I said, laughing. "That's where the story sort of dries up."

"Well, butter my buns and call me a biscuit."

"What on earth are you talking about?" I said, glancing over at her.

"It's a Southern expression to indicate surprise," she said. "It's one of my mom's favorites."

"Oh, I thought it was just another way for you to express hunger," I said.

"I could eat."

"I'm shocked."

"You know, Rooster's one of the strangest people I've met in a long time, but I feel good about giving him one of the Shepherd pups," Josie said.

"Yeah. It'll be the most pampered pooch in town."

Chapter 12

For the next few days, Josie and I went back and forth about how to overcome the logistical challenges involved in tailing two purported smugglers who were using a boat on the St. Lawrence River in the middle of December to carry out their crimes. We refused to even be on the water during what I called the Tweener Season; the time of year when the River was still deciding between transitioning into a 750 mile long ice-bath, the world's largest ice skating rink, or a mini-glacier that swallowed the shoreline and extended out into deeper water as far as the cold, wind and snow allowed. In short, the River was especially dangerous this time of year and one small mistake, like running into even a small stretch of ice in the dead of night, could send you overboard to a certain early, frigid death.

Besides, we had already put our boat into winter storage and had the perfect excuse for not following the Baxter Brothers. At least following them from the water. It was Josie who first had the idea that, even if we couldn't actually follow the pair from the water, if we could somehow pinpoint their destination we might somehow be able to observe them from land.

We then headed for the Clay Bay library to do a little historical research on the bootlegging that had operated in the area during Prohibition. More specifically, we were on the hunt for any information about the Baxter Brothers' infamous grandfather, Monroe Baxter. We each gathered an armful of books and sat down across from each other at a small table in the empty reference room.

I spent the next fifteen minutes flipping through a long, but somewhat sketchy overview of the area during Prohibition and found no mention of

Monroe. I glanced up to reach for another book and noticed that Josie was completely hidden from view behind a stack of books that surrounded her on three sides. Impressed by her focus on the task before us, I was about to compliment her when I heard a mouse-like crinkle of paper, followed by the unmistakable sound of her chewing. I peered over the stack of books and saw her turning pages with one hand, and using her other hand and her teeth to open bite-size Snickers.

She'd already found her rhythm.

Turn the page, select one of the treats from the bag, tear, pop and chew, read, turn the page.

Lather, rinse, repeat.

She paused mid-chew when she saw me staring at her over the stack of books.

"Well, would you look at who went and built herself a little fort," I whispered.

"Libraries always make me hungry."

"You're not supposed to have food in here," I said.

"I know," she said. "That's why I built the fort."

"Unbelievable," I said. "Is that leftover Halloween candy?"

Josie raised an eyebrow.

"Sorry, dumb question," I said.

Around our place, there was no such thing as leftover Halloween candy. In fact, over the years, local trick or treaters had learned the hard way about the need to stop by our house early in the evening.

"The store was having a Halloween clearance sale, so I loaded up," Josie whispered. "You want one?"

"Well, maybe just one," I said, glancing around for any sign of Ms. McTavish, our local librarian who was one of the sweetest people in town, but a total stickler when it came to library rules and quick to punish offenders.

Josie reached into her coat pocket and tossed me a fresh bag.

"I didn't mean one bag," I whispered.

"Suit yourself. More for me," she said, popping another bite-sized morsel. "Hey, I think I've got something."

I carefully slid the bag of Snickers into my pocket and moved my chair to her side of the table. I shook my head at the collection of strewn candy wrappers. Josie pointed down at the book she was reading.

"There's a whole chapter here on Monroe Baxter. There's even a photo."

I studied the black and white photo of a large hairy man smiling and holding a case of Canadian whiskey. The resemblance to his grandsons was remarkable.

"An adventurous but odious and violent man with no regard for either the law or social norms, Baxter was well-known and feared throughout the area," Josie said, reading from the book.

"Ivy Lea is mentioned a lot of times," I said.

"That's the nice little hamlet with the boathouses and cottages just on the other side of the River, right?" she said, popping another piece of candy into her mouth.

"Yeah, and it was a major smuggling spot during Prohibition," I said.

"You think the grandsons might be following in old Monroe's footsteps? Maybe trying to pay him some sort of weird tribute?"

"Could be," I said. "But what is really interesting about that area is that the River narrows quite a bit near Ivy Lea and the current is really strong around there."

"And that would keep the water from freezing, right?"

"Yes, it certainly does," I said. "Smuggler's Cove is around there."

"Smuggler's Cove?" Josie said. "I'm assuming that's a spot that was aptly named."

"Yeah, it leads right to shore at the edge of a big campground that's there now. And there are a lot of small islands around there that made good places in the old days to hide if the Feds were on the prowl."

"It would be pretty remote this time of year," Josie said.

"Yeah," I said, continuing to scan the page.

"If we knew when the Baxter Brothers' boat left Rooster's place, we could get there by car in about twenty minutes," Josie said.

"Sure. Once we clear Canadian Immigration, we make a left, and it's just up the road. Or we could just roll the dice, find a good spot to hide, and wait for them to show up," I said, already rolling several possible options around in my head.

"We should probably call Jackson and let him know what we're doing," Josie said.

I considered the idea, then shook my head.

"I'd rather wait until we have a better idea of what we're dealing with. Maybe the Baxter Brothers just have girlfriends on the Canadian side."

"Yeah, right," Josie said. "And I'm the local rep for Weight Watchers."

"Look, if we call Jackson, he'll call the locals on the Canadian side and probably the state police. And if the Baxter boys give a whiff of the cops, they might just take off."

"Would that be so bad?" Josie said, laughing.

Her laugh elicited a loud, long shush from Ms. McTavish who was hovering near the entrance to the reference room.

"Sorry, Ms. McTavish," I said, waving to her.

Josie collected all the empty wrappers, stuffed them into the bag, and slowly slid it into her pocket.

"I hear she likes to confiscate if she catches you," Josie whispered.

"The rumors are true," I whispered. "She's a big confiscator."

Ms. McTavish had once busted me when I'd snuck some fudge brownies into an after-school reading group. Since I was eight at the time, I'd gotten off with a warning. But I did lose the brownies.

And to this day, I swear I'd smelled chocolate on her breath later on my way out.

Chapter 13

"Two pairs of binoculars?"

"Check," Josie said.

"Two flashlights?"

"Check."

"Notepad and pen?"

"Check."

"Thermos of tomato basil soup?"

"Check."

"Thermos of hot chocolate?"

"Check."

"Two ham and cheese baguettes?"

"Uh, we're one short."

I gave Josie the evil eye, and she shrugged.

"Don't worry," she said. "The other one has your name on it."

"A dozen brownies?"

"Close enough."

"Large can of mixed nuts?"

"Relatively speaking," she said.

"You're unbelievable. We better hit the road before you work your way through the whole basket."

I turned off the overhead light and backed the SUV out of the driveway. Through a stiff breeze and light snowfall, we headed across the various spans of the Thousand Islands Bridge system that connected the U.S. and Canadian sides and made our way through Canadian Immigration in record time. A few minutes after nine, we pulled into the empty campground and found a place to park in a strand of pines that provided both a hiding place and a good view of Smuggler's Cove. I turned off the lights but left the car running and the heater on.

Not taking any chances, I made Josie take the first watch while I polished off my ham and cheese baguette.

"Man, it would be freezing out there on the River," Josie said, scanning the horizon for signs of boat lights.

"Yeah, it wouldn't be fun," I said. "I hope whatever the Baxter Brothers are smuggling is worth the pain and suffering."

We both heard the sound of another vehicle and hunched down as it drove past us about a hundred feet to our right.

"Interesting," I said, reaching for my binoculars. "It's a panel van."

"Yeah, but I can't tell if there's any writing on the side," Josie said.

"Dark."

"Good work, Sherlock."

"Just watch the water," I said, continuing to peer through my binoculars at the van.

Whoever was inside obviously didn't have plans to leave their warm vehicle any more than we did.

"Here we go," Josie said with a touch of excitement in her voice. "Straight down, right in the middle of the water."

"Got it," I said.

"All I can make out are the running lights," she said.

I squinted through the binoculars, but all I could see were the green and red lights on the bow and a bright white light extending from the stern.

"We really need night vision goggles for something like this," I said.

"Maybe Santa will bring you a pair," she said, laughing.

I thought about it and decided I'd gotten worse Christmas presents in prior years.

"Okay, they're on the dock," Josie said.

Two flashlights came on and our ability to see improved.

"That's our guys," Josie said.

"What's that they're carrying?" I said.

"I can't tell," she said. "They're covered up. Call me crazy, but they look like dog carriers."

"Don't tell me they're running more than one puppy mill," I said. "These guys are so going down."

We watched the Baxter Brothers walk along the path that led from the dock and up a small hill. When they were a few hundred feet away from the van, a lightbulb went off in my head.

"I'll be right back," I whispered, making sure the overhead light was turned off before I opened the door.

"Where on earth are you going?" Josie whispered, pausing from her surveillance to watch me.

"To the dock."

"What?"

"I'll be back in two minutes," I whispered. "Just keep an eye on them."

I partially closed the door and shivered as the cold and wind hit me. I hunched low and made my way through the pines, and started down the hill. Then I tripped over a small stump that was buried by the snow, tumbled and rolled three times, then landed face down in a snowdrift about four feet deep. I stifled a groan and worked my way into a standing position, brushed the pine needles off my face, and shook the snow out of my ears. It was an extremely painful, but relatively quiet fall and no one had seemed to hear it. As important was the fact that Josie hadn't been around to see it.

If she had, I'd never hear the end of this one.

I limped the rest of the way down the hill, knowing that I'd probably gashed my right knee. But I remained focused and made my way to the dock where I tiptoed through the dark until I reached the Baxter Brothers' boat.

I took one more look back up the hill but couldn't see more than a few feet in front of me and decided I was safe from prying eyes. I climbed onto the boat, headed for the stern, and then leaned over until I found what I was looking for. The jolt of cold I received when I reached my hands under the water took my breath away. I quickly unscrewed the two drain plugs from the back of the transom and dropped them in the water. Immediately, I heard the soft gurgle of water entering the boat.

Trying not to laugh out loud, I climbed out of the boat back onto the dock and limped my way back up the hill through the pines and back to the car. I climbed in and gently closed my door. Josie stared at me like I'd lost my mind.

At the moment, despite the fact that I was gasping for breath, I had to admit that I did feel a bit like an evil genius. While I waited to get enough air back into my lungs to speak, I decided to count my adventure down to the boat and then back up the hill as two workouts. It was a good thing I'd gotten both of them in, since the way my knee was throbbing, I was probably about to go on the disabled list.

"What did I miss?" I said when I was finally able to talk.

"The Baxter Brothers delivered four puppies," Josie said. "I saw them when they opened the back of the van, and the light came on."

"Did you get a look at the guys they delivered them to?" I said, picking up my binoculars.

"Yeah, but I've never seen them before," Josie said. "But I did get the number of their license plate."

"Good job," I said. "Jackson can help us out with that. What else?"

"They gave the Baxter Brothers a stack of cash," Josie said.

"They're going to need it," I said, laughing.

"What?"

"I'll tell you later," I said. "Hey, the guys in the van are leaving."

"You want to follow them?" Josie said.

"No, not tonight," I said. "I need to get home and have you take a look at my knee."

"What's the matter with your knee?"

"I sort of fell down the hill," I said, embarrassed.

"Sort of?" Josie said. "Are you okay?"

"Yeah, it's just a cut. But I might need you to give me a couple of stitches."

"You do know that I'm not licensed to work on people, right?" Josie said.

"Who am I going to tell?"

"Yeah, I guess you have a point there," Josie said. "Was it a good fall?"

"Oh, yeah. I got a 9.5 from the Russian judge," I said, managing a small laugh.

"And I missed it?"

"Yeah, lucky me."

We watched the van turn around and drive off. We waited until we saw the lights of the Baxter Brothers' boat disappear, and then headed for home. We munched brownies in silence for several minutes and then I glanced over at Josie.

"What kind of puppies were they?" I said.

"Labs. Three yellow and one chocolate. About eight weeks old."

"Were they in bad shape?"

"That's what was weird about the whole thing. The puppies were perfect."

"Really?"

"Yeah. From what I could tell, all four were healthy and happy."

"What the heck are we dealing with here, Josie?"

"I have no idea."

Chapter 14

Around ten the next morning, I was in the condo area in the back of the Inn saying hello to all the dogs when Jackson poked his head inside the door.

"There you are," he said. "Got a minute?"

I slowly climbed to my feet and gently removed three of the Cocker Spaniel puppies from me in the process. Limping, I led Jackson to my office.

"Are you okay?" he said as he watched my labored effort.

"Yeah, I'll be all right," I said, wincing. "I just banged up my knee a bit."

Josie was already in the office sitting on the couch and digging through a ceramic Santa for the last of the Christmas cookies. She came up empty, frowned as she put the top back on the cookie jar, and placed it on the desk.

"Remind me to take that up to the house later," Josie said, nodding at the ceramic Santa. "It needs to be reloaded."

Jackson poured himself a cup of coffee and sat down across the desk from me.

"I just got some interesting news I thought you'd find funny," he said, removing his Chief's hat and setting it on the desk next to his coffee.

"What's up?" I said, rubbing my tired eyes.

I'd gotten to bed around two and hadn't slept well. After we'd gotten home, Josie led me into one of the exam rooms where she cut the leg of my jeans off above the knee and got her first look at my wound.

I was okay with her cutting up my jeans. If I didn't soon take drastic measures, I wouldn't be able to fit into them anyway. And if I did manage to drop a few pounds, they'd make great cutoff shorts for the summer.

When life hands you lemons, right?

Josie scowled when she first saw the cut. But after she cleaned away all the blood, it wasn't as bad as we both originally thought. She gave me a shot to numb the area and used five stitches to close the wound. I worried aloud that I might end up with an ugly scar, but Josie said there was no need for me to worry; the scar would be beautiful. Then she'd snorted and laughed way too long.

I owed her one for that crack.

"I got a phone call this morning from Rooster Jennings," Jackson said, taking a sip of coffee.

"How's Rooster doing?" I said, glancing at Josie.

"The same," Jackson said. "He asked me to swing by his place and take a look at something."

"What was it?" I said.

"Well, the first thing I saw were the Baxter Brothers wrapped in blankets and being transported to the hospital where they're undergoing treatment for hypothermia. Then I saw their boat on its side under the water; get this, while it was still tied to the dock."

"How about that?" I said. "Well, we always knew it was just a matter of time before they won a Darwin award."

Josie snorted.

"According to the Baxter boys, they took their boat out for a ride last night, did some drinking and who knows what else, then returned and parked at the dock. They decided to have another beer before heading home, but they fell asleep. Around seven this morning, they woke up when their boat, now full of water, flipped over on its side, sunk, and tossed both of them into the River," Jackson said.

All three of us roared with laughter.

"The drain plugs had been removed," Jackson said. "And neither one of them has a clue how that happened."

"Good," I said.

Jackson gave me an odd stare. Since we needed Jackson's help tracking down the license plate number from last night, we told him the whole story. He listened carefully, jotted down a few notes, and even laughed from time to time. He laughed a little too hard when I explained how I'd ended up with five stitches in my knee.

"Taking those drain plugs out was pretty clever," Jackson said. "But the Baxter boys were lucky they kept moving on their way home. If they'd decided to drift for a while, they could have sunk in the middle of the channel."

"Can't win them all," Josie said, removing a fresh bag of the bite-sized Snickers from her lab coat.

When Josie said she'd stocked up, she wasn't kidding.

I'd known that as long as the Baxter Brothers had kept moving, the lack of drain plugs wouldn't create any problems given the inclined angle a boat has when moving at speed. Any water inside the hull would actually drain from the boat as they drove home. The problem would come when the boat was just sitting in the water. I'd hoped that their boat would sink while still tied to the dock in Ivy Lea, but this outcome was even more enjoyable.

"How long do you think it will take to find out the owner of that van?" I said.

"About as long as it will take Josie to finish that bag of Snickers," Jackson said, laughing.

"Funny," Josie said through a mouthful of chocolate.

Jackson scrolled through his phone, found the number, and placed the call. Seconds later, he greeted the person on the other end and recited the number of the license plate. He sipped his coffee as he waited. Less than two minutes later, Jackson jotted down the information he was being given, then thanked the person and hung up.

"It's a corporate account," Jackson said. "But that van's address is in Kingston."

"It's a pet store, isn't it?" I said.

"You got it in one," he said, sliding the piece of paper across the desk.

"Happy Family Time," I said, glancing down at it.

"I know them," Josie said. "It's a franchise operation based in Toronto. I see them in the vendor hall all the time at conferences and trade shows."

I opened my laptop and searched for the company's website. I scanned a couple of pages.

"One hundred twenty-two stores across Canada," I said. "A woman named Virginia Alexander is listed as owner and CEO. Does her name ring a bell?"

Josie and Jackson both shook their head. I glanced at Josie.

"Are you up for a drive?" I said.

"Kingston? Why not?" Josie said. "My schedule is clear today. And we can stop for lunch at that great Chinese restaurant."

"Oooh, yeah. Good call," I said.

"Hey, guys," Jackson said. "Maybe it's time for you two to take a step back and let the cops handle it."

"What are they supposed to handle, Jackson?" I said. "All we know is that the Baxter Brothers delivered four dogs last night. And the only thing this pet store might be guilty of is smuggling puppies across the River. How hard do you think your cop buddies on the Canadian side will laugh when you ask them to investigate that?"

Jackson considered the question, then nodded.

"Pretty hard, probably," he said. "But there has to be a connection to Jerome's murder somewhere in this, right?"

89

"I think it's definitely possible," I said. "Do you think you can get anything out of the Baxter Brothers?"

"Nah, they won't talk to me," Jackson said.

"Put them back in the water and they might," Josie said, finally pushing the bag of Snickers out of reach.

Chapter 15

Less than an hour from Clay Bay by car, Kingston is located where the St. Lawrence River meets Lake Ontario and the Rideau Canal. It's a stunning setting, and the city of around 125,000 is one of my favorites. We casually drove around town enjoying the historical buildings then found the pet store and Chinese restaurant we were looking for. Since it was almost noon, we decided to eat first. I parked in front of the restaurant, and we hopped out and looked around the bustling downtown streets that were brightly decorated and crowded with shoppers.

"It has kind of a Norman Rockwell feel to it," I said.

"Sure. If old Norman were Canadian," Josie said.

"You got a point there," I said, laughing. "You know, I heard that Kingston was recently named one of the top seven most intelligent communities in the world."

"No wonder the Baxter Brothers didn't want to make the drive," Josie said, heading for the front door.

We ate until we were stuffed to the gills and almost embarrassed by the stunned looks we were getting from the wait staff. They boxed up our leftovers, and we made our way back to the car and drove to the pet shop a few blocks away.

"How do you want to play it?" Josie said.

"Let's just play it straight," I said. "We're looking to buy a puppy."

"Okay," Josie deadpanned. "We should be able to pull that off."

"Funny," I said, opening the front door.

A young girl in her teens greeted us warmly.

"Hi, I'm Charlotte. Can I help you find something?" she said.

"Yes," Josie said. "We're thinking about getting a puppy for one of our nieces."

"What a nice Christmas present," Charlotte gushed.

"We thought so, too," Josie said, smiling back at her.

"What kind of dog were you thinking about getting her?"

"Probably something big," I said. "Like a Lab."

"Oh, that's too bad," Charlotte said, frowning. "I don't think we have any Labs at the moment."

"Gee, they went quick," Josie whispered.

I gently punched her in the arm and looked at the young girl.

"Are you sure?" I said. "Maybe there was a recent delivery you weren't told about."

"Gee, I don't think so," Charlotte said. "But I guess it's possible. I'm only working here part-time through the holidays."

"If you could check, that would be wonderful," I said.

"Let me go grab Mr. Jones. He's the owner."

We watched her stroll toward the back of the store.

"Sweet kid," Josie said.

"Yeah," I agreed, then glanced down and saw the beagle puppy staring up at me from inside the metal pen stretched out across the floor. "Well, what do we have here?"

The beagle cocked its head and wagged its tail furiously. I bent down and picked him up.

"What a soft touch," Josie said, laughing.

"He's adorable," I said, cradling the puppy to my chest.

"He certainly is," Josie said. "I wonder if he's the last one left from his litter."

"If he is, then the rest of his siblings must have been drop-dead gorgeous," I said, nuzzling the puppy.

"Mr. Jones will be right out. I see you've met Barney," Charlotte said as she approached. "He's something else."

I handed the puppy to her, and it was immediately apparent they were old friends.

"It looks like the two of you have bonded," Josie said.

"Oh, we have," Charlotte said, laughing as the puppy licked her face. "I'd love to be able to keep this guy."

"Why not?" I said.

"Oh, I could never afford him," Charlotte said. "He's seven hundred dollars."

I glanced at Josie, who blinked at the number. We weren't fans of pet stores and the exorbitant prices they sometimes charged, and seven hundred dollars would feed a lot of dogs. But it wasn't the puppy's fault he'd ended up here and, to quote Josie, a well-placed dog today is one less rescue tomorrow.

A stout, middle-aged man approached and extended his hand.

"Jimmy Jones," he said, shaking both our hands. "I understand you're looking for a dog as a Christmas present for one of your nieces."

"Yes," I said. "Preferably a yellow or maybe a chocolate Lab."

"Sorry," he said, shaking his head. "I don't have any at the moment. And it's been a couple of months now. I'm expecting some after the New Year, but that doesn't really help you out now."

"No, it doesn't," I said, frowning at Josie.

"Do you have any idea where we might find one?" Josie said.

"Gee, I guess you could check the other stores in town. Maybe check the classified ads in the paper. You just never know what you're going to get if you go that route. It's sad to say, but there are some nasty people out there selling dogs."

"So we've heard," I said, glancing at Charlotte who was still snuggling with the beagle puppy. "Tell me about this little guy."

"Barney? Oh, he's a great dog. He's the last one of his litter. I can't believe he's still here." Then he smiled and winked at us. "I can't be sure, but I think Charlotte has been hiding Barney out back every time someone comes in."

Charlotte turned red with embarrassment.

"Mr. Jones," she said. "I never."

"Just kidding with you, Charlotte," he said, laughing.

"You know, Josie, I think our niece would just love Barney," I said.

"Are you out of your mind?" Josie whispered.

"Relax."

"Forty-seven isn't enough?" she muttered under her breath.

"We'll take him, Mr. Jones," I said, glancing at Charlotte who was on the verge of tears.

"That's great," Mr. Jones said. "Now, if you'll just follow me, we'll get all the paperwork taken care of and you and your new pup will be on your way. I'll need your full name and address for the registration."

I looked at Charlotte.

"You heard the man, Charlotte," I said. "Give Mr. Jones your full name and address."

"What?" she said, stunned. "You're joking, right?"

"Charlotte, I never joke about dogs," I said, rubbing the puppy's head before handing him to her. "Merry Christmas."

Charlotte squealed with delight, hugged me, then Josie, and then for good measure, kissed Mr. Jones on the cheek. Barney, sensing good news, barked loudly. I handed the stunned Mr. Jones a credit card and five minutes later we were on our way out the door.

"You're unbelievable," Josie said as we walked to the car.

"I have my moments."

"Well, that was definitely one of your better ones," Josie said.

"Thanks," I said, climbing into the car.

"Do you think Mr. Jones was lying to us?" Josie said.

"No, I don't."

"Me neither. That means that someone on the staff is using his van to smuggle puppies," Josie said.

"Yeah. That's what I was thinking," I said, focusing on the road.

"That's what you were thinking?"

"What if the people borrowing the van don't work for him at all," I said. "Maybe Mr. Jones works for them."

"You mean the corporate people who sold him the franchise rights?" Josie said.

"Yeah. How weird is that idea?" I said, glancing over at her.

"It's pretty weird," she said. "But by your standards, it's not that crazy."

I laughed and set the cruise control to sixty-five when we reached the highway.

"All of a sudden I'm feeling the Christmas spirit," I said. "I was beginning to wonder if it was going to show up this year."

"Well, if buying a seven-hundred-dollar puppy for a complete stranger doesn't do the trick, nothing will," Josie said.

"I need to finish up my shopping," I said.

"Me too. We're running out of time," Josie said, pulling a fresh bag of the bite-sized Snickers from her coat pocket.

"You're like a squirrel hiding nuts to eat later," I said, nodding at the bag.

"Hey, it's a long winter," she said, holding the bag out for me. "Just wait until you see what I've got stashed in the pantry."

I laughed then fell silent as I looked through the windshield at the light snow that had begun falling.

"What do you want for Christmas?" I said eventually.

"Anything you get me will be just fine, Suzy," she said, then turned her head and stared at me. "Except a dog."

Chapter 16

After completely whiffing on our attempt to link the four puppies the Baxter Brothers had transported across the River to the van owned by the Happy Family Time pet store in Kingston, I went back to my research on the corporation and its head office in Toronto. It was a decent sized company, but nothing extraordinary by any means. The company's history briefly mentioned a planned, but ultimately abandoned, attempt to expand into the U.S. For the last several years, growth in the number of franchises had been flat, and the company's marketing literature came across as a soft-sell at best. I thought it was odd that a company based on a franchising model wasn't more aggressive, but perhaps their current strategy was to maintain, not grow.

Maybe they were satisfied with the size and profitability of the corporation.

Maybe they weren't capable of expanding the number of franchises without investing a ton of money to support the new growth.

Maybe they were in a holding pattern on the pet store side until another business opportunity came along that would let them move in a different direction. That thought stuck with me, and I stayed with it for about half an hour before I abandoned it.

Maybe the whole thing was a simple as the fact that a Happy Family Time staff member had crossed paths with the Baxter Brothers and come up with a way to supplement their incomes by smuggling dogs across the border.

But if that were the case, then why had the puppy mill we'd found been in such disrepair with a couple dozen dogs close to death? If I were running a sandwich shop, I wouldn't be buying rotten tomatoes to serve on three-day-old bread.

I remembered the chicken salad sandwiches with walnuts and a basil-dill mayo on fresh sourdough that Chef Claire had mentioned she was making for lunch, but fought through my hunger pangs and focused on the task at hand.

I scanned the entire list of Happy Family Time franchisees and found several that were within driving distance of Kingston. My new working theory, or as Josie called it, my latest wild goose chase, was that someone from the pet store in Kingston had borrowed the store's van, picked up the puppies from the Baxter Brothers, dropped them off, and then returned the van before the store opened the next morning.

If the puppies had been dropped off at another of the Happy Family Time stores, I knew that I had a decent shot of identifying which one at some point. But if the puppies had been delivered anywhere else, my theory was shot, and I'd have to start over. And starting over meant interacting with the Baxter Brothers. As you might imagine, I was rooting for my Happy Family Time theory to hold water.

At least more water than the Baxter Brothers' boat was holding at the moment.

I know, I know. It's not nice to gloat.

But I was allowing myself an exception for that pair of dog abusers.

And since I was giving myself a pass, I still laughed every time I thought about their boat sunk and laying on its side while still tied to Rooster's dock.

I headed for the back of the Inn to see how everyone was doing and found Josie, Sammy, and Jill playing with the Cocker Spaniel puppies in their condo. Since early fall, we'd gone back to our core staff that consisted of the four of us. Usually, we managed to stay busy throughout the winter, but around the holidays things tended to slow down even more, and we were in the middle of a lull. I certainly didn't mind because it meant that I got to spend most of my day hanging out in the condos playing with the dogs.

The cocker puppies were doing great and all of them, except Tripod, had already been adopted and were scheduled to be handed over to their new owners on Christmas Eve. Several people had expressed an interest in the three-legged puppy who continued to amaze all of us with how quickly he was overcoming his challenge. But Josie and I had big plans for Tripod and politely refused any and all adoption offers.

"How's everyone doing?" I said, sitting down next to Josie.

One of the puppies immediately hopped into my lap, and I picked her up and held her close as she licked my face

"They're little furry balls of fun," Josie said, laughing as she fended off two of the puppies vying for her attention. "They'll be ready to go soon."

I nodded and watched Sammy roll a ball across the condo. Tripod hopped his way toward the ball, grabbed it in his mouth, and returned. He dropped the ball in Sammy's lap and wagged his tail furiously as he waited for the next round.

"Did you make any progress?" Josie said.

"Tons," I said.

"Liar."

"I've got it narrowed down," I said.

Josie snorted.

"To what? Somewhere on the Canadian mainland?" she said.

"No," I snapped. "Ontario. Maybe Ottawa. There are two Happy Family Time stores in Ottawa."

Josie thought about my comment and then, to her credit, managed a nod.

"Well, if we believe your theory, and I don't, someone could have easily driven from Kingston to Ottawa and returned the van before the store opened."

"Yeah, it would be a piece of cake," I said, then silently chastised myself.

"Hmmm," Josie said. "Hey, Sammy. Would you mind doing a Paterson's run at lunchtime?"

"Sure," Sammy said. "You want the usual?"

"Yes please," Josie said. "But also grab one of their chocolate cakes while you're there. Just put it on my tab."

"You got it," Sammy said.

People ran tabs at their favorite bar. Josie was the only person I knew who had one at a bakery.

"You're unbelievable," I said, shaking my head.

"Me? It was your idea."

"What on earth are you talking about?"

"Who's the one who mentioned cake?"

Knowing I'd lost, I let the conversation go and focused on the black ball of fur now sleeping in my lap.

"We need to go to Ottawa and check out those two stores," I said, stroking the puppy's head.

"Would it be worth my energy to try and talk you out of it?" Josie said.

"You know better than that. Of course not."

Josie nodded and then nuzzled the two puppies before glancing at me.

"Say, I have an idea, Suzy," Josie said. "Let's drive to Ottawa and check out those two pet stores."

Chapter 17

We made the drive from Clay Bay to Ottawa the next morning in less than two hours. Since we'd eaten a hearty breakfast that had even left Chef Claire staring at us in disbelief, we decided to check out the two stores before worrying about refueling. The first store was a complete waste of time and not a pleasant experience. I doubted if the leaders of the Happy Family Time company had visited the store in recent years. It was located in a rundown strip mall on the far edge of the city, was filthy, and devoid of animals. The shelves were virtually empty, and the owner was an unpleasant man who spent the entire ten minutes we were there on the phone with his bookie scratching various body parts and whispering vague promises about making a payment on what we decided was a rather large gambling debt.

"That was pleasant," Josie said as we headed back to the car.

"Yeah, I need a shower. I guess he could be the sort of guy who might get involved in smuggling," I said.

"Maybe," Josie said. "But not dog smuggling."

"Unless they were Greyhounds," I deadpanned.

"Oh, good one," Josie said. "Dog racing and bookies. I get it."

"No need to get snarky," I said, checking my phone for driving directions to the second store.

We had better luck there. The place was large and clean with a friendly staff and a lot of animals of all types and sizes. The dog area contained a variety of breeds of different ages and we repeated our cover story about wanting to buy a Lab for our niece.

"I'm sorry, but we're out of Labs at the moment," the young man supervising the dog section said. "But we do have two Golden Retriever puppies from a recent litter."

I glanced down into the fenced area and saw the two puppies wrestling with each other on the floor. I started to reach down when I felt my arm being pulled back.

"No," Josie snapped. "You pick one of those up, and you'll be toast."

"But just look at them," I said.

"I'm doing my best not to," she said, laughing. Then she turned to the young man. "Would it be possible to talk with the owner about when he's expecting to get some more Labs?"

"Sure, I guess," he said, shrugging.

We watched him disappear into the back of the store, and a few minutes later a middle-aged man approached.

"Hello. I'm Bill Waters. Jeff tells me you're interested in a Lab puppy," he said, beaming at us.

His eyes lingered on Josie. It wasn't an overt leer, but I knew he'd had to stop himself.

"Yes, for our niece," I said. "We'd like to give her the puppy for Christmas, but we're having a hard time finding one that's ready to go."

"Yeah, that can be tough this time of year," he said.

"Have you had any lately?" Josie said.

He stared at Josie for several seconds before responding. I wasn't sure if her question had touched a nerve or if he was just getting around to leering at her.

"Yeah, I had four that came in the other day, but they were all pre-sold," he said, shrugging.

"Do you think you could give us the number of the breeder?" I said. "Maybe they have still some left from that litter."

My question caught him right between the eyes and he glanced around the store as he tried to compose a suitable response.

"Uh, I doubt if there are any left. The four I got were beautiful, and I'm sure they all went fast," he said.

Josie took a step toward him and put a hand on her hip. She brushed the hair back from her face and released a full-on charm assault on the unsuspecting man. She didn't do it often, but when she did it sure was fun to watch.

"What kind of Labs were they?" she whispered.

"Three yellows and a chocolate," he stammered.

"Oooh, I love chocolate labs," she cooed.

"Yeah, me too," he said, unconsciously flicking his tongue over his upper lip.

"How old were they?" she whispered breathlessly.

"Eight weeks," he said. "Same as always. They come in ready to go. They're even already chipped."

"It sounds like you made an excellent choice going with that breeder," she said, again touching his arm.

"Well, sure," he stammered. "Nothing but the best for the dogs, right?"

"Of course. Are you sure the breeder doesn't have any left?" Josie said, pouting her lips like a disappointed young girl.

"Well, I guess I can't say for certain," he said.

"Would you mind taking a few minutes to give them a call?" Josie said, gently placing a hand on the man's arm. "We'd be so grateful."

The man swallowed hard and then nodded his head several times. For a moment, he reminded me of a bobblehead doll.

"I'd be happy to," he said.

We watched him walk to the back of the store and disappear from sight.

"Be careful," I said, laughing. "He might have a bad heart."

"Do you think it's odd that the puppies are already micro-chipped before they're delivered?" Josie said.

"No, I don't think it's that unusual. We put chips in all the time."

"Yeah, but we have the owner's information available when we do it," Josie said.

"He said they were all pre-sold. All he would need to do is give the info to the breeder, and they could enter it in the dog registration system and print out the owner certificates."

"Yeah, you're right," Josie said, shrugging. "Never mind. False alarm."

"Three yellows and a chocolate," I said. "Think it's a coincidence?"

"Not a chance," Josie said.

"You think this guy is dirty?" I said.

"Yeah, I think so," Josie said. "But let's not make a final decision until we see what he has to say."

"Good thinking," I said, noticing him heading back toward us. "Here he comes. Whatever you do, go easy on him."

"I was thinking about showing a bit of cleavage," Josie said.

"I wouldn't," I said, laughing. "You might kill the poor guy. Besides, I don't think you'll need it."

He stopped a few feet away from us and spoke to Josie.

"I'm sorry," he said. "But they're all gone. Apparently, I got the last four."

"Oh, I can't believe we missed out," Josie whispered. "It sounds like they were great puppies."

Josie put her hands on her hips and posed as she stared off into the distance.

"Perfect," he mumbled.

I suppressed a laugh.

"Would it be possible to get the breeder's number?" I said.

He looked at me and seemed surprised to see me. I assumed he'd forgotten I was even there.

"Uh, I don't know," he said, stalling. "This particular breeder is pretty private and only deals with a handful of select sellers."

"Like you, right?" Josie said, again placing her hand on the man's arm.

"Well, you know," he said, his face turning red. "What can I say? I take great pride in the dogs I sell."

"I understand completely," Josie said, her pouty lips on full display. "If I were a local breeder, I wouldn't even consider dealing with anyone else."

"Oh, he's not local," the man blurted before catching himself. Then he must have decided that revealing the location didn't matter. "They're down in Kingston."

"Well, you must take our number and be sure to give us a call the next time a litter is ready," Josie said, finally removing her hand.

"Oh, I will," he said, again doing the bobblehead thing. "Maybe I'll give you a call just for the heck of it."

"I'd love that," Josie said.

She slowly removed the pen from his shirt pocket and wrote a number on his hand. He glanced down at it, then beamed at Josie.

"Well, I guess I'll be seeing you around," he said.

"Oh, you can bet on it," Josie said, flashing him a big smile.

"You know," he said, doing everything he could think of to prolong the conversation, "I've been waiting on a litter of Cocker Spaniels. I haven't gotten an update lately, but I'd be happy to check. Great dogs."

"Yes, they are," Josie said, glancing at me. "But we're looking for a bigger dog."

"Well, if that's the case, are you sure I can't interest you in one of those Golden puppies?" he said.

"Actually," I said, taking a step toward the dog area.

I stopped short when Josie grabbed my hand.

"We'd love to," she said, staring directly into his eyes while continuing to apply the death grip to my hand. "But our niece really has her heart set on a Lab."

"I understand," he said, then waved goodbye and walked away staring down at the phone number Josie had written on his hand.

We left the store and headed for the car.

"You almost broke my hand," I said, massaging it.

"You got off easy," she said. "You would have bought both of them, wouldn't you?"

"Maybe."

"Unbelievable," she said.

"Whose number did you give him?"

"My Uncle Fred's office number in Georgia," Josie said, laughing.

"The one who works for the FBI?"

"Yup," Josie said.

"You're too much, I said. "What do you want to do now?"

"I could eat."

"Really?"

"Fake flirting always makes me hungry."

Chapter 18

The microchip used to help identify lost dogs is about the size of a grain of rice and is implanted under the skin between the shoulder blades via a quick injection. Some people think the chips work like a Global Positioning System where the animal can be tracked, but GPS requires a battery and, therefore, the two systems are very different. The microchips that are implanted in dogs have one function; storing a unique number used to identify the pet's owner.

When a lost dog is found, a scanner can be moved over the skin and, if a chip exists, the scanner reads the microchip's unique ID number. Once that number is identified, either an online search or a call, placed to the company that maintains the registry database, will obtain the owner's contact information.

We have one of the scanners and use it all time. We also implant the chips often and are very familiar with the enrollment process. The enrollment form includes a lot of information. In addition to the chip ID, the form included the owner's contact information, a description and name of the dog, and other information such as the name of the dog's vet and an emergency contact person.

All of that information would be very helpful to us. We just had one little problem. We didn't know any of the ID numbers of the four dogs. Without that, it was impossible for us to conduct our own search.

This was the problem we were trying to solve over pizza, salad, and wine.

Josie reached for another slice of pepperoni and mushroom. I decided to stick with the onion and sausage. Having learned the hard way about getting in our way when we were eating, Chef Claire waited patiently until we finished refilling our plates, then served herself.

"It's pretty good pizza," she said.

"Yeah," Josie said. "But nothing like you're going to be serving at the new restaurant."

"No, it's not," Chef Claire said.

She stated it a simple statement of fact, delivered in a no-nonsense manner devoid of ego. It was one thing to be really good at your craft; it was something else altogether to let your work speak for itself and not feel compelled to tell the world how good you were. Chef Claire shared that trait with Josie who consistently avoided talking about her abilities as a vet, and I continued to be amazed that our small town had been able to secure the services of two people as talented as Chef Claire and Josie. The fact that they, respectively, were experts in food and dogs, the two things I had the most passion about, reinforced the fact that the life I lived was charmed.

At the moment, Josie was feeling less than an expert in her chosen field. It had taken her a while to accept my theory about the dog smuggling operation, but now that she had, she was all in and wracking her brain to figure out a way to get her hands on the four ID numbers of the Lab puppies. As she ate, she continued to stare off into space deep in thought. I decided to let her eat in peace.

"So, what's new on the Jackson and Freddie front?" I said to Chef Claire.

"Nothing," she said, shaking her head. "Their pretty bruised at the moment and keeping their distance."

"That's what you wanted, right?" I said.

"Yeah, I guess," she said. "But Christmas is coming, and I don't want any bad feelings to spoil it. Regardless of how this turns out, they're still my friends, and I want to keep it that way."

"Don't worry," I said. "Jack and Freddie know they screwed up, and, to their credit, are willing to admit it. And they don't hold grudges. It's just a matter of how long you want to keep them in the penalty box."

Chef Claire laughed and took a bite of salad.

"So which one are you most attracted to?" I said.

"I have no idea."

"Well, you got all winter to make up your mind," I said, glancing at Josie who was still staring off into the distance as she chewed.

"The renovations are going great," Chef Claire said. "The kitchen equipment was delivered yesterday, and we should have it installed by the end of next week."

"That's great," I said.

"And wait until you see the wood-burning pizza oven they're building," Chef Claire said.

"Pizza oven?" Josie said, coming out her trance. "What was that about a pizza oven?"

We both laughed.

"Earth to Josie," I said.

"Sorry for drifting off," she said. "But I think I have a good idea."

"I already told you, Josie," Chef Claire said. "You can order whatever toppings you want."

Again we laughed, and Josie made a face at us.

"Funny," Josie said. "I think I know how we might be able to get our hands on that information."

She got up from her chair and left the kitchen. A few minutes later she returned carrying a stack of business cards. She sat back down, put a piece of crust in her mouth and chewed as she flipped through the cards.

"I know he gave me one of his cards," Josie said.

"Who?" I said, grabbing a slice of the pepperoni and mushroom.

"Here it is," she said, holding up one of the cards. "Jeffrey Cavendish. And, yes, he's as stuffy as his name sounds. But he's a total dog lover."

"Who is he?"

"I met him at a conference in New York last year. He did a presentation about some Canadian animal coalition he runs in Ottawa. And one of the things his organization does is to help maintain the national dog registry database."

"Well done," I said.

"I only agreed to take one of his cards to get him to leave me alone," Josie said. "Now I'm glad I did."

"Did he come on to you?" I said.

"Yeah, but the way he did it was pretty creepy. Everywhere I went, he was always lurking."

"So he's a lurker?" I said.

"No, he's not that creepy. He's more of a hoverer," Josie said.

"A hoverer?"

"Yeah. He's a big time hoverer," Josie said, grabbing her phone.

"I hate hoverers," I said.

"Me too," Chef Claire chimed in.

"Six o'clock on a Friday," Josie said. "I don't like our chances of catching him in the office. I'll just leave him a message."

Josie dialed the number, and to our surprise, a British-accented voice answered on the third ring. I had to admit that, despite the fact he was a hoverer, I liked his voice.

"Jeffrey Cavendish speaking."

"Hi, Jeffrey. It's Josie Court. You're certainly working late on a Friday. I thought I'd get your voicemail."

We heard silence on the other end of the line, but seconds later it became clear that the name had finally registered.

"Josie," he gushed. "I was just on my way out, but what a nice surprise to hear from you. How are you?"

"I'm great, Jeffrey," Josie said.

"Is this a business or pleasure call?" he said. "Not that it matters, of course."

Sure, Jeffrey. We believe you.

"Well, let's say it will be my pleasure to do business with you," Josie said.

"Fair enough," he said, laughing. "How can I help you?"

Josie spent a few minutes explaining the puppy mill we'd stumbled on, the dog smuggling, and what we were trying to do. She left out the part about Jerome getting shot in the forehead. Jeffrey might be enamored with the prospect of hooking up with Josie, but he might draw the line at somehow getting caught up in a murder case.

I thought it was a good call on her part.

"Despicable people," he said. "What can I do?"

"I was wondering if it was possible for you to give us temporary access to your national database," Josie said.

"No, I'm afraid I can't do that, Josie," he said. "That would be a breach of our policy. And since I wrote the policy..."

"Yeah, I get it," Josie said. "I knew it was a long shot."

"But I'm fully within my rights to do whatever searches I see fit," he said.

"You're so good, Jeffrey," Josie said.

"You have no idea," he said.

Josie glanced at both of us and shook her head in disgust.

Major whiff, Jeffrey.

"We're trying to locate four Lab puppies that were probably chipped sometime last week. Or maybe early this week. And it sounds like they probably went to homes in Ottawa. They were sold by the Happy Family Time store downtown if that helps."

"I'm very familiar with Happy Family Time. And I think I've even been in that store. This shouldn't be too hard," he said. "Give me a minute."

Josie munched on a slice while we waited. He came back on the line.

"Sorry, Josie. I don't have any Labs being registered with chips during that time period," he said.

Josie and I exchanged frowns.

"Could you remove all the date parameters and run it again just to see if anything comes up?" she said.

"Sure," Jeffrey said.

Again, we waited.

"Here we go," he said. "Four Lab puppies were chipped and registered today. Three yellows and a chocolate."

"Today?" Josie said. "That's odd."

"And all four dogs have the same vet listed as the emergency contact," Jeffrey said. "What are the odds of that?"

"I'd say they were pretty long," Josie said. "Who's the vet?"

"The one and only Dr. Perry Long," Jeffrey said.

"Perry Long?" Josie said.

"The veterinarian to the stars," he said, laughing. "At least that's the way he describes himself."

"He does have a bit of an ego, doesn't he?" Josie said, laughing along. "Would it be possible for you to email me all the particulars?"

"If it might help bust up a puppy mill operation, I'm more than happy to do that. And the next time you get up to Ottawa, we simply must get together for dinner. Or even lunch."

Josie squirmed in her chair like a fish flopping on a dock. But she was trapped, and she knew it.

"Jeffrey, I'd love to have lunch with you," she said eventually.

"That's great," he said. "I know the perfect spot. They have an Indian buffet that will take your breath away."

"I'm looking forward to it," Josie said.

They said their goodbyes and Josie put her phone away.

"Indian food. Buffet. And Jeffrey," she said. "I guess two out of three isn't bad."

"He can't be that bad," I said, laughing.

"Let's see if you still have the same opinion after you meet him," Josie said.

"What are you talking about?"

"You're coming with me," Josie said.

"No way."

"Yes, Suzy. I'm not going by myself. And you heard the man. Indian buffet. You love Indian food."

She was right. I did.

I nodded and took a sip of wine. Josie gave me an evil grin and focused on what was left of her dinner.

"You're going to owe me big time for this one," I said.

"What else is new?" she said, winking at Chef Claire.

Beaten, I grabbed another slice of the sausage and onion.

The things I do around here.

Chapter 19

We had a lot of information to process, and we spent the next morning when we were making our rounds trying to make sense of it. After our conversation had circled back on itself for the third time, we decided to take a break and headed for my office. Jackson was already waiting for us and sitting on the couch with his feet propped up on the coffee table reading a magazine. Josie sat down next to him while I poured coffee for all three of us then sat down behind my desk.

"I'm glad you called," Jackson said, tossing the magazine aside. "I needed a break from the murder case."

"What have you found out?" I said.

"I've got bupkus," he said, sipping his coffee. "We know the Baxter Brothers are definitely smuggling dogs, and they're probably the ones who were operating that puppy mill, but as far as the night of the murder goes, their alibi checks out. They were playing poker with a couple of buddies most of the night. So I'm left with no suspects, no murder weapon, and no motive."

"The motive had to be that someone wanted to shut Jerome up for divulging the existence of the puppy mill," I said.

"Suzy, we've been through this," Jackson said, his voice rising a notch. "By calling you, we know that's what Jerome was doing, but we don't have a clue if anybody else knew it. He could have been killed for another reason altogether. And it might have nothing to do with the dogs."

"What other theories do you have?" I said.

"Like I said earlier, I've got bupkus. But thanks for the reminder," he snapped.

"Then until you do have something, Officer Fife, I'm going to stick with my theory if that's okay with you," I said, glaring at Jackson.

"Watch yourself, Suzy," Jackson said.

"Guys, please," Josie said. "You're giving me another headache."

Jackson and I continued to glare at each other before breaking eye contact and settling back into our seats.

"So what have you guys been up to?" Jackson said.

"Apparently, a lot more than you," I said.

"Suzy, please. Dial it down," Josie said, turning to Jackson. "We have the names of the four people who got the Lab puppies."

"And?" Jackson said.

"They're all upstanding citizens who live in Ottawa," Josie said. She paused for a moment before continuing. "And they all have the same vet."

Jackson frowned.

"Doesn't that sound kind of strange to you?" he said.

"At first it did," Josie said. "The vet, Dr. Perry Long, is incredibly successful and is known for taking care of the pets of rich and famous. His clients include most of the top politicians, athletes, and corporate leaders. He advertises a lot on television, writes books, and has his own agent and publicist. He's become a celebrity in his own right and having him as your pet's vet has become sort of a status symbol."

"Weird," Jackson said.

"Yeah, a little," Josie said.

"Well, if you don't mind," Jackson said, patting Josie's knee, "I think I'll stick with the celebrity vet I already have."

"Aren't you sweet," Josie said, holding out her coffee mug to toast Jackson.

"Besides, Sluggo would never forgive me if I changed vets," he said, laughing.

"How's my favorite Bulldog doing?" Josie said.

"He's great."

"Hey, guys," I said. "How about a little focus here? The meeting of the mutual admiration society can be held later."

"Somebody's grumpy this morning," Jackson said to Josie.

"You know how she gets when she can't solve a mystery. Plus, she can't figure out what to get her mom for Christmas," Josie said, taking a sip of coffee. "And she's freaking out about gaining four pounds."

"Hey, I told you that in confidence," I said, glaring at Josie.

"Oops," she said, laughing.

"Really? Four pounds. Where?" Jackson said.

Josie snorted and almost spilled her coffee.

"That is absolutely none of your business, Jackson," I snapped.

"No, I meant that I can't imagine where you gained it. You look fantastic," Jackson said.

"Nice save," Josie whispered.

"So tell me a bit more about this vet," Jackson said, anxious to change topics.

So was I, but I continued to glare at him as a reminder to stay away from that particular subject.

"Well, like I said, he's incredibly successful and is very active on the social scene. Animal rights, the arts, all the usual suspects," Josie said. "And he has a reputation for being a total player."

"Has this guy ever hit on you?" Jackson said.

"Only every time he sees me," she said, laughing. "I occasionally see him at meetings and conferences. We do our usual dance, and then he goes on his way. He's a bit annoying, but generally harmless."

"It still sounds suspicious that he ended up being the vet for all four of those dogs," Jackson said.

"Yeah, it does," Josie said. "But the owners are all heavy hitters in the corporate world or high-ranking government officials. Since they all probably travel in the same social circle, it's plausible."

"You mentioned a couple of the Happy Family Time stores," Jackson said. "What's the deal with them?"

"We think they're definitely involved in some way," I said. "The one in Kingston is probably a key player in the logistics of the smuggling operation. That's probably your best leverage with the Baxter Brothers since we saw that with our own eyes."

"That reminds me," Josie said. "I need to take a look at your knee today."

It was nice of her to remember. I smiled at her, then nodded and continued.

"The Happy Family Time store in Ottawa handled the delivery of the puppies. They might have also handled the sale, but my guess is that those deals were done long before they arrived at that store," I said.

"I still don't understand why they need to smuggle in puppies from the States," Jackson said. "I'm sure Canada has more dogs than they know what to do with."

"They were pretty cute dogs," Josie said.

"Have you ever seen a Lab puppy that wasn't?" I said.

Josie shook her head as she reached for the candy jar on the desk.

"They have to be smuggling something in the puppies," I said. "But what on earth could that possibly be?"

"Not to mention the question of what they could possibly smuggle inside puppies that didn't run the risk of killing them?" Josie said. "And if we ever find out that they've killed some, they're going to find themselves in a world of hurt."

"Definitely," I said.

117

"But why would they go to all that trouble to smuggle them in and run the risk the dogs might not make it through the process?" Jackson said.

"Yeah, that's what we keep circling back to," I said.

"It doesn't seem to make any sense to put something in an eight-week-old puppy's stomach," Jackson said.

"I agree," Josie said. "But I've been wracking my brain and can't come up with anything else."

A lightbulb went off in my head, and I stared off into the distance.

"You've got that look," Josie said. "What is it?"

"We've been coming at it all wrong," I said.

"What are you talking about?" Jackson said.

"Hang on," I said. "I need a minute to think this through."

They continued to stare at me like I'd lost my mind.

I didn't mind. I was pretty used to it by now.

"Are the Baxter Brothers out of the hospital yet?" I said.

"Yeah, they've been out for a while," Jackson said.

"Have they got their boat dried out?" I said.

"Yes, I swung by Rooster's yesterday and the boat is back in its slip and apparently as good as new."

"It's Thursday," I said.

"So?" Jackson said.

"So it's one of their scheduled delivery nights," I said.

"And you think they're going to keep going with whatever they're up to?" Jackson said.

"Why would they stop?" I said. "As far as they know, all they had was a mishap with their drain plugs. And knowing them, they're probably blaming each other for forgetting to put them in. But nobody, including you as the Chief of Police, asked them anything that would make them suspicious, right?"

"I was too busy laughing to ask them any questions," Jackson said. "So what do you expect me to do? Follow them tonight and arrest them?"

"No, not at all," I said. "It's way too early to arrest the Baxter boys. But it would be good if you could find out what dogs are being smuggled in tonight and then give us a call. And as soon as you do, we'll be on our way to Ottawa."

"We will?" Josie said.

"Yes."

"To do what?" Josie said.

"To steal a dog. What else?"

"Oh, of course," Josie deadpanned, staring at me. "Dumb question on my part."

Chapter 20

We got the call from Jackson around ten, and by midnight we were checking into the Westin in Ottawa, a great hotel that was minutes from pretty much everything downtown Ottawa had to offer. But given the late hour and our early morning plans, we decided to go low-key and settled for snacks and a nightcap in the hotel bar.

Sammy had been like a little kid at Christmas the entire drive, but he'd finally settled down and was now nervous, wondering if he'd be able to pull off the morning charade we had planned. He settled for a beer and some peanuts as he watched us each devour a club sandwich and double order of fries.

"Let me guess," he said, laughing. "Stealing dogs always makes you hungry."

"First of all, Sammy," Josie said. "I believe the term you're looking for is rescuing. And the club sandwich is an insurance policy just in case we miss breakfast in the morning."

"What she said," I mumbled through a mouthful of fries.

"Are you sure this is going to work?" Sammy said.

"Absolutely not," Josie said, shaking her head. Then she caught the look of panic on Sammy's face. "Relax, you're going to do just fine."

"But what if I get caught?" Sammy said.

"Doing what? Impersonating a dog smuggler?" Josie said.

"Yeah, I guess you've got a point," he said, shrugging. "So what do you guys want for Christmas?"

"A global dog park," I said.

"Oooh, good one," Josie said, laughing.

"No, really," he said. "I have no idea what to get you guys. I can never repay you for all you've done for me."

"Tell you what, Sammy," I said. "You pull this off tomorrow, and we'll call it even. How's that?"

"Fair enough," he said, smiling. "So who am I supposed to be?"

"We're still working on that," I said, shrugging.

Sammy's smile faded.

In the morning, Sammy's smile still seemed a bit forced when we parked down the street from the Family Happy Inn pet store. The store opened at nine, and our plan was to get there early before any other customers arrived.

"What's the owner's name again?" I said, leading the way to the store.

"Bill Waters," Josie said.

"Right," I said, coming to a stop about a hundred feet from the front door. "Okay, Sammy, give us ten minutes then come in and ask for Bill Waters. Tell him what you want, and if he pushes back at all, hang tough and use what we gave you."

"Okay, I think I've got it," he said. "And if he doesn't buy it?"

"Run like hell," Josie deadpanned.

"You're not helping," I said, glaring at Josie.

"Sorry. Sammy, if it doesn't go well, just turn indignant, tell this guy Waters that you'll be back, and storm out of the store."

"I can do that," Sammy said. "Ten minutes, right?"

"See you then," I said, heading for the store. "You think he's going to be able to pull it off?"

"I guess we're going to find out soon enough," Josie said.

We entered the empty store and saw the owner near the cash register. He glanced up, recognized Josie immediately and grinned.

"Well, look who's here?" he said, heading toward us.

"Hi, Bill," Josie said, beaming at him.

"Hi, Josie. You couldn't stay away, huh?" he said.

"You got it in one, Bill," Josie said, placing a hand on his forearm.

Then he glanced at me.

"Hi there. Gwen, right?"

"Suzy."

"Right. Suzy," he said, snapping his fingers. "How are you doing?"

"I'm fine," I said. "We thought we'd stop back and see if you still had the Golden puppies."

It was a great excuse for us dropping by his store again, and I congratulated myself when it worked to perfection.

"No, I'm sorry," he said. "I sold the last one yesterday."

"We dodged a bullet there," Josie whispered.

"Oh, I'm so sorry to hear that," I said, giving her a quick evil eye.

"But I did just get in a couple of beautiful Springer Spaniels," he said.

"Oooh, I love Springers," I said.

"Well, let me go bring them out," he said. "I'll be right back."

"Suzy, I'm warning you," Josie said. "We're here to steal a dog, not buy one."

"It can't hurt to look while we're waiting, can it?"

"Unbelievable," she said.

We both turned around when we heard the door open. Sammy entered and started to casually stroll toward us. The owner returned carrying an adorable spaniel puppy in each arm. He handed one to both of us, then focused on Sammy. I stared down at the puppy that was looking up at me with the most beautiful brown eyes I'd ever seen. I glanced at Josie who was fixated on the puppy she was holding. Then she shook her head as if coming out of a trance and gently placed the puppy inside the spacious gated area.

122

She took the puppy I was holding and soon the two spaniels were rolling around on the floor playing.

As instructed, Sammy had stayed within earshot of us.

"Good morning," the owner said to him.

"Hi. They were right," Sammy said, glancing around. "It's a really nice store you have here."

"Well, thanks," Waters said. "Who are they?"

"The folks I work for," Sammy said. "I'm here to pick up their new dog. Scooter's in meetings all day, and Bunbuns is headed for Montreal to do some Christmas shopping."

"Scooter and Bunbuns?" Waters said, scratching his head.

"Well, those are their nicknames that everyone close to the family calls them," Sammy said. "But how would you know that, right?"

Good one, Sammy. Got him right between the eyes.

"I'm sorry, but I'm going to need a bit more information," Waters said.

"Like what?"

"Well-"

"Look, I've already had to move my schedule around to take care of this. And I have a ten o'clock vet appointment with Dr. Long. And if I'm late, then it will probably be at least a couple of weeks before I can get it rescheduled. And if the dog doesn't get its exam today, I'll be toast with Scooter and Bunbuns. If you catch my drift. Or if you prefer, I can just make a call to the capital and explain the situation to some of our friends down there."

"No, no. There's no reason for that. No need to get the folks on the other side of the border involved."

Josie and I stared at each other. Sammy blinked but didn't lose his focus.

"I'm glad to hear that," Sammy said, sneaking a quick glance in our direction.

"If you can just tell me the breed of dog and its name, I'm sure I'll be able to help you."

"It's an eight-week-old Newfoundland who goes by the name of Captain. He has a little patch of white on the bridge of his nose," Sammy said.

"That's the one," Waters said, smiling. "Let me go get him, and you'll be on your way."

"Thank you. I really appreciate it," Sammy said.

Sammy exhaled loudly and walked toward the area where the two spaniels were still rolling around.

"I thought I was going to wet myself," Sammy whispered.

"Hang in there," Josie whispered. "You're doing great."

"Tell that to my bladder."

The owner returned carrying the puppy. It was black except for the tiny patch of white Jackson had mentioned over the phone last night. Sammy held the puppy in one arm while he scribbled his signature on the piece of paper Waters was holding out. Sammy folded the receipt and put it into his pocket, shook hands with the owner, and nodded goodbye to us on his way out the door.

"Now, what do you think of the Springers," Waters said, focusing on us.

"Gorgeous," I said.

"Yes, they are," Josie said. "But our niece has her heart set on a big dog. That Newfie would have been perfect."

"I'm sorry, but that was the only one I got. And as you probably noticed, he was pre-sold."

"Well, we just thought we'd stop by and say hello," Josie said.

"I'm so glad you did. I was actually about to give you a call on my offer to take you to lunch," he said. "Don't you dare go and forget about that."

"Oh, don't worry, Bill," she said, placing a hand on his arm. "I'm sure I'll remember."

We waved goodbye and walked quickly toward the car. Sammy was waiting and cradling the puppy in his arms. We climbed in, and I headed for the highway. About twenty miles south of Ottawa, my breathing returned to normal.

"That was intense," Sammy said, handing the puppy to Josie in the passenger seat. "And what was his comment about getting the people on the other side of the border involved? When I mentioned calling the capital, I was talking about Ottawa."

"I know. That was strange," Josie said, holding up the puppy for a quick inspection. "Hello, Captain."

"What are you going to do with him?" Sammy said.

"I'm going to give him a very thorough check up," Josie said. "After that, he's all mine."

"You're joking, right?" I said, not believing what I was hearing.

"I've always wanted a Newfie. And this little guy is perfect," Josie said, snuggling the black ball of fur. "Aren't you, Captain? Oh, and Sammy?"

"Yeah."

"Don't worry about getting me anything else for Christmas."

Chapter 21

Between our rescue of the Newfie puppy, Captain, and the fake papers Josie had created for the dog that worked like a charm on our way back across the border, I was forced to admit to myself that we if we hadn't crossed the line, we were certainly straddling it. I know a few sticklers will insist on calling our efforts to rescue the smuggled puppy stealing, and I don't even want to think about how many laws we might have broken smuggling Captain back across the border.

We'd brought the puppy back to the Inn, and I checked in with the rest of the dogs in the condos before joining Josie in one of the exam rooms. Five minutes later, I was on the phone with Jackson. A half hour after that he arrived accompanied by Detective Abrams from the state police. Now, the four of us were sitting in my office waiting for our lunch order to be delivered.

Josie was on the couch with Captain stretched out on her lap. The puppy's tongue was hanging out of his mouth from the belly-scratch Josie was administering. It was apparent to me that the connection between Josie and her new companion was already strong and soon would be indestructible. Jackson watched Josie's fingers dance up and down the dog's stomach and laughed.

"Think he'll be following you around much?" Jackson said.

Detective Abrams shook his head as he watched the puppy's reaction.

"I know I would," he said, laughing. Then he glanced at Josie as if afraid his comment was out of line. "Sorry. Brain cramp."

Josie laughed and stroked the puppy's head.

"Don't worry about it," Josie said. "But you do need four legs to get one of these."

"Story of my life," Detective Abrams said. "Okay, I know you didn't invite us over just to eat sandwiches. What's up?"

I started by providing a summary of how we'd stumbled onto the Baxter Brothers involvement in the dog smuggling ring. When I got to the part about how their boat had sunk while tied to the dock with the brothers still in it, I had to wait for Detective Abrams to stop laughing before I continued. Then I continued with our research into and subsequent visits to the Happy Family Time stores.

Detective Abrams listened carefully and scribbled notes as I talked. Jackson then explained how we'd identified Captain during the Baxter Brothers latest smuggling run. He'd gotten a good look at the puppy when it had been put in the back of the van, and I made a mental note to ask Jackson what kind of binoculars he had. It appeared that they were even more powerful than my own.

There was a knock on the door and Jill entered carrying a box that contained our lunches. She set it down on the desk.

"Did you guys order for yourselves?" I said, examining the contents.

"Yeah, we're all set," Jill said. "Thanks for doing that."

"No problem," I said. "Enjoy."

"The Water's Edge pastrami? I'm sure we'll be just fine," Jill said, laughing as she left the office.

"Since when did the Water's Edge start serving pastrami sandwiches?" Detective Abrams said, reaching for one of the sandwiches.

"Ever since Chef Claire gave Millie her recipe," Jackson said.

As we ate, I finished the story with an overview of how we'd gotten our hands on Captain that morning and made it back to the Inn.

"So, you stole the puppy?" Detective Abrams said.

"Technically, we think it's more of a rescue," Josie said.

"Technically?" Detective Abrams said, raising an eyebrow.

"Yes," Josie snapped, clutching the puppy.

"Relax, Josie," Detective Abrams said. "Nobody is taking your dog. As far as I'm concerned, you got the puppy somewhere in New England. But let's call a spade a spade."

"I'll agree to call it a rescue-steal," she said. "How's that?"

The two cops in the room both laughed, and Josie relaxed.

"So that's it?" Detective Abrams said. "You had a guilty conscience and wanted to get it off your chest?"

"No, we called you because of what we found after we got home," I said, reaching into my shirt pocket and removing a small envelope. I slid it across the desk. "Be careful. It's tiny, and I almost dropped it earlier."

Detective Abrams pushed the sides of the envelope apart and looked inside. He frowned and glanced back and forth at Josie and me.

"What is it?" Jackson said, peering over the detective's shoulder.

"It's a microchip," Detective Abrams said, then looked at Josie. "Where did you find it?"

"It was implanted in Captain," Josie said.

"Aren't microchips used all the time with dogs?" Jackson said.

"Yeah, but not this kind of chip," Detective Abrams said. "This is something you'd expect to find on a computer."

"When we got home, I examined Captain to make sure he's okay. The first thing I did was use our scanner to see if he had a chip installed. The owner of the Happy Family Time store in Ottawa told us that the dogs from that breeder come to him with a chip already implanted. But the scanner didn't pick anything up. I thought I felt a small spot where an incision was made, but couldn't be sure just using my hands, so I decided to do an x-ray. Lo and behold, there it was just below the back of his neck. I used a little numbing agent on the little guy and was able to cut it out in a few seconds. The chip appears to be wrapped in some sort of plastic to protect whatever is on it."

"The poor little guy is eight week's old and has already been cut on two times," I said, shaking my head.

"I wouldn't worry about it," Jackson said, taking a bite of pastrami. "I'm sure he'll forget all about that when Josie gets around to neutering him."

"Jackson!" Josie and I shrieked.

"Hey, I'm just saying," he said, shrugging.

Jackson had a good point, but that didn't stop us from glaring at him for the next few minutes. Detective Abrams took a bite of his sandwich and chewed in silence before speaking again.

"You said the owner of the pet store mentioned the people on the other side of the border when Sammy mentioned the capital," he said.

"Yeah," I said. "We assume he meant Washington, but it doesn't make any sense to us."

"It seems like kind of a stretch," Detective Abrams said. "That's a long way to transport a dog and then smuggle it across the River. If I were coming from Washington, I'd use a private plane and fly directly to Ottawa."

"But they'd still have to go through Customs and Immigration, right?" Josie said.

"It didn't stop you, did it?" Detective Abrams said, laughing.

"Yeah, you got a point there," Josie said, a hint of a smile forming in the corners of her mouth.

"But as soon as he heard Sammy say, capital, he jumped like he'd stuck his finger in a light socket. Where else could cause a reaction like that?" I said, picking up the other half of my sandwich.

"I don't know," Detective Abrams said. "Albany?"

129

I stopped just as I was getting ready to take a bite and put my sandwich down as a lightbulb went off in my head and burned brightly.

"Wow," I said. "How about that?"

"What is it?" Detective Abrams.

"I have no idea," Josie said. "But it made her drop her sandwich, so I'm betting it's something big."

I made a face at Josie, then fell silent.

"The guy in Albany at the security company," I said.

"Yeah, Fullerton," Josie said. "What about him?"

"He promised to call us when he figured out why Jerome's cell phone had never been turned off."

"That's right," Josie said. "He did."

"But he never called," I said.

"No, he didn't."

"Maybe he just forgot," I said.

"Or maybe he thought we'd just forget all about it," Josie said.

"We did," I said.

"At least until this moment," Josie said.

"Yeah," I said. "Didn't Fullerton say that his ex-wife was a well-known expert and consultant to a bunch of technology companies in Tech Valley?"

"He certainly did," Josie said.

"And you guys are now thinking that these people in Albany are using dogs to smuggle computer secrets across the border?" Jackson said, wiping mustard off his face.

I looked at Josie who thought about Jackson's question, before nodding at me.

"Yes," I said. "I guess that's exactly what we're saying."

"I doubt if that microchip is filled with their favorite recipes," Josie said.

Detective Abrams sighed loudly and tossed what was left of his sandwich onto his plate.

"I knew a quiet Christmas with the family was too much to ask for," he said.

He stood up and headed for the door.

"Where are you going?" Jackson said.

"I need to make a few calls," he said, then glanced back and forth at us. "Nice job, ladies. Now please do everyone a favor and extricate yourselves from the process. Thanks for lunch."

"No problem, Detective Abrams," I said. "And I'm sorry we ruined your Christmas."

"Don't worry about it," he said on his way out the door. "It was bound to happen."

"Extricate?" I said.

"Yeah," Jackson said. "It means to remove or untangle."

"I know what it means, Jackson," I said, frowning. "I just can't believe he felt the need to mention it."

"Because you've already decided to let this thing go? Or he was just wasting his breath when he said it?" Jackson said.

"That second thing you said," Josie said, laughing.

"I don't know, folks," he said. "If this involves corporate espionage, there's a lot of money at stake. And things could turn ugly in a hurry."

"We're sorry, Jackson," I said. "But who knows what else they might be doing to dogs? You saw the condition of the ones we rescued from that puppy mill were in. For us, this one is personal."

Jackson, deep in thought, sat back in his chair and munched on a pickle. He glanced over at Josie who continued rubbing the now sleeping puppy's stomach.

"Look at the size of the paws on that guy," Jackson said. "How big is he going to get?"

"He'll probably top out near a hundred and fifty when he's full grown," Josie said.

"Big dog," he said. "Nobody is going to be messing with you, right?"

"Nobody messes with me now, Jackson," Josie said, flashing him a smile.

"I think we should pay Dr. Perry Long a visit," I said.

"You know, I was thinking exactly the same thing," Josie said.

"Okay, guys," Jackson said. "You've done more than enough. I'm sure Detective Abrams appreciates all your help. But you need to back off. I have to say it again. This could get dangerous for you two in a hurry."

"Jackson, you know perfectly well that most of the work the cops do is going to focus on the theft of computer secrets. They won't spend five minutes on what, for them, is a small-time dog smuggling operation."

"Maybe," Jackson said. "But how is this vet, Dr. Long, going to help you?"

"It looks like he's on the receiving end of all the smuggled dogs," Josie said. "And he's probably the one who's removing the computer chips. But maybe he's an innocent player in all of this. We're just going to have a little chat with him."

"Gee, Josie," Jackson said. "Why don't I believe you?"

"Easy," I said. "Shared history."

We all laughed.

"Okay, but I need to go along with you," Jackson said.

"No, Jackson," I said. "That would be too much of a red flag."

"Then I'll wait in the car while you talk to him," he said. "I'm sorry, but this one isn't up for negotiation."

Josie and I glanced at each other before nodding our agreement.

"Thanks for not fighting me on this one," Jackson said. "Now for the hard part, what excuse are you going to use for dropping in on him?"

That was a good question.

Man, these cases always wear me out. There are too many questions and so many details to sort out.

The way things are going, I'll never get my Christmas shopping finished.

"I guess I could ask him for some advice on a medical problem with one of our dogs," Josie said.

"That would be a hard sell, Josie. He knows how good a vet you are, and we don't want to do anything to make him suspicious," I said.

"Maybe you could take Captain into his office and see what sort of reaction the guy has. You know, confront him with some direct evidence, turn up the heat, and try to smoke him out."

Josie and I both stared at him like he was from another planet.

"We just got Captain away from those monsters, and now you want me to put him right back in the middle of it?" Josie snapped.

"What is wrong with you, Jackson?" I said, my eyes flaring.

"Geez, guys. Relax. I'm just spitballing here," he said, polishing off the last of his sandwich.

"Well, don't," Josie said.

"What she said."

We sat quietly for several moments before Josie snapped her fingers.

"I've got it," she said. "I'll call Dr. Long and ask him if he'd be willing to take a look at our expansion plans and offer some input."

"Perfect," I said.

In the spring, we'd be breaking ground on a project that would more than double the capacity of our rescue program. And while we were both delighted with the final architectural plans, asking a renowned vet for his advice was the perfect cover story.

"And what makes you think that he will open up to you?" Jackson said.

"Because I'm going to flatter his enormous ego and use every ounce of charm and guile I can manage to summon without throwing up in his office," Josie said.

Jackson nodded.

"Speaking from personal experience, the poor guy doesn't stand a chance."

Chapter 22

"If we keep crossing the border like this, pretty soon Canadian Immigration is going to make us honorary citizens," Josie said.

"Or get suspicious and start asking you a lot of questions," Jackson said from the back seat.

"Who invited him?" Josie said, laughing.

"I invited myself," Jackson said. "Somebody has to keep you two out of trouble."

Very familiar with the route to Ottawa, I set the cruise control to seventy and stretched my legs out. I noticed the odometer was about to pass another major milestone and realized a new car was definitely in my future.

"Two hundred thousand miles," I said, nodding at the odometer.

"Wow," Josie said. "We were both a lot younger when you got this."

"And I was a lot lighter," I said, glancing over at her. "I gained another pound."

"Relax," Josie said. "It's the holidays. And you look great."

"At this rate, I'm going to need a new wardrobe," I said. "I need to do something."

"I'd tell Santa," Josie said. "I hear he's good handling things like that."

"Funny."

We left the highway and followed the directions on Josie's phone to Dr. Perry Long's clinic that was located in an upscale suburb not far from the city. We pulled into the crowded parking lot and found a spot near the entrance. Jackson handed Josie a small metal object.

"What's this?" she said, examining the object.

"It's a transmitter," Jackson said. "If I can't go inside with you, I'm at least going to listen in on the conversation."

"Jackson, nothing is going to happen inside his clinic," Josie said.

"I'm glad to hear that," he said. "Then just consider me extremely nosy. Pin it somewhere on the collar of your coat where it won't be easy to see."

Josie did as Jackson instructed and we got out of the car, stretched our backs, and looked around. Judging from the size of the clinic and the parking lot that resembled a foreign car dealership, Dr. Long was doing very well.

"Why would he risk everything to get involved with a smuggling ring?" I said, heading toward the front door.

"Well, people usually do stupid stuff for money, power, or sex," Josie said.

"It looks like he's got plenty of money," I said.

"It sure does," she said. "He's got quite a set up here."

"I like our place better," I said, holding the door open for her.

"Me too," she said as she headed for the receptionist.

We confirmed our appointment and sat waiting for the famous Dr. Long. But he was everywhere we looked. A couple of dozen framed posters of him posing with various dogs adorned all four walls of the waiting area. He soon appeared in a doorway and posed with his hands on his hips, beaming at Josie.

"Josie!" he called from the other side of the room. Then he strode toward us and pulled Josie in for a hug.

It wasn't a bone-crusher, but probably hard enough to dislodge the transmitter and I scanned the floor just in case. Josie freed herself from his clutches and smiled at him. He was very good looking, a fact he was well aware of, tall, and in great shape. Beneath his monogrammed white lab coat, he wore a periwinkle sweater, jeans and a pair of running shoes that matched his sweater. I doubted it was a coincidence and decided he probably had a closet full of matching sweaters and sneakers.

"This is my business partner, Suzy Chandler," Josie said.

"Of course," he said, grasping my hand. "The other half of the infamous Doggy Inn I've heard so much about."

"Nice to meet you, Dr. Long," I said.

"Oh, call me Perry," he said, flashing me a wide smile before refocusing on Josie. "You look fantastic."

"Thanks, Perry," Josie said. "And we appreciate you taking the time to review our expansion plans."

"I'm honored that you asked, and I'm delighted to help," he said. "It sounds like an exciting project. Let's go to my office."

We followed him into a massive office that contained an ornate wooden desk, floor to ceiling bookshelves, and two leather couches. We sat down on one, and he settled in behind his desk and beamed at us. More photos of him with people I assumed I should recognize filled one of the walls. Then I saw the photo on his desk and nudged Josie with my foot. She glanced at the photo of Perry and a woman with their arms around each other on the 18th tee at Pebble Beach.

"Isn't that Fullerton's ex-wife?" Josie whispered.

"Yup," I whispered as I pulled the architectural plans from my bag.

I spread the plans out on Perry's desk, and he stood up to study them.

"Okay, I see what you're doing," he said. "My, your dogs must certainly be happy there. Look at the size of those individual living areas."

"We call them condos," I said.

"I can see why," he said, laughing.

I had no idea if this guy's interest was genuine or if he was a total con artist, but I found myself warming up to him.

"Okay," he said, running a finger across the plan. "You're going to tie into the existing structure right here, and come off at a ninety-degree angle and run the new section along the back edge of your play area." He glanced up at me. "How big is your play area?"

"Two acres," Josie said.

"I'm envious," he said. "I'd kill for that much room. I have to make do with half an acre."

"It doesn't look like your dogs are suffering, Perry," Josie said, leaning in close to him.

"No, they're not," he said, placing a hand on top of Josie's.

Josie patted his hand with her other one, then smoothly slipped away to take in the office.

"This is nice," she said. "Suzy, we should think about doing something like this in our offices."

"Let me know if you do," Perry said. "I'll give you the contact info for the guy who does all my work."

"Thanks, Perry," Josie said, beaming at him. "You're so sweet."

"Don't tell anybody," he said, winking at her. "You'll ruin my reputation."

We both forced a laugh. Josie's sounded a lot more natural than mine.

"Business must be good if you're doing a renovation this size," he said, glancing down at the plans.

"Yeah, we stay pretty busy," Josie said. "And we're constantly chasing our tails trying to keep up." She flashed him a coy smile. "Get it? Chasing our tails?"

"Oooh, good one," Perry said, reaching out to touch Josie's forearm. "I forgot how funny you were."

"And don't even get me started on the number of rescues we're trying to deal with," she said, shaking her head.

"Tell me about it," Perry said. "It's tragic what some people do with their dogs."

"I know," Josie said. "Just the other day, somebody dropped off the most beautiful Newfoundland puppy on our doorstep."

"You don't say," Perry said, trying too hard to sound casual.

"Yeah, the poor little guy," Josie said.

"Is he okay?" Perry said, sitting down and staring at Josie.

"Yeah, he's fine," Josie said, sitting back down on the couch and crossing her legs. "But I can't figure out why he's constantly trying to rub and scratch the back of his neck."

"Really?" Perry said.

"It's odd," Josie said. "I've checked the area out, but I can't feel anything. If he keeps it up, I'm afraid I'm going to have to do some x-rays on Captain to see what's going on."

"Captain?"

"Yeah, that's his name," Josie said. "He had a tag on his collar with his name, but that was it. There wasn't any contact information anywhere." She shook her head. "Some people, huh?"

"Yeah, some people," Perry said, frowning. "You say the dog was just dropped off at your front door?"

"Yes. One of our staff heard whimpering, and when she opened the door, there he was."

"And you didn't see who dropped him off?" Perry said.

"No. Why?" Josie said, casually leaning back on the couch and playing with her hair.

Perry couldn't miss her overt flirting, but he seemed preoccupied with other thoughts at the moment. He fidgeted with his pen, then managed to make eye contact with Josie.

"Well, because whoever did something like that should be in jail. Don't you agree?"

"Oh, I agree completely, Perry," Josie said. "So what do you think about our plans?"

"Uh, they're great," he said, rolling them up and handing them to me. "I wouldn't change a thing. Remember to invite me to the grand opening."

"Oh, I do hope you'll be able to make it," Josie said, getting up off the couch.

"Say, I have an idea," he said. "Maybe I'll swing by before you start the renovation."

"Perry, you know you're welcome to visit anytime," Josie said. "But why would you want to do that?"

"Well, and bear with me while I try to think and talk at the same time, but I have a lot of contacts in the publishing industry, and I think a lot of people would enjoy reading a feature article on your rescue program."

"You really think so?" Josie said breathlessly as she took a step toward him.

She sat down on the edge of the desk and stared down at him.

"You would do something like that for us?" Josie said.

"Of course," he whispered. "Anything for you, Josie."

"I'm going to owe you big time for this, Perry," she said, bordering on the edge of saccharine.

Jackson had been right; the guy didn't have a chance.

"I think we should do a before and after feature. I can swing by with my photographer and take some shots now. Then we'll come back once the renovation has started, and again when the project is finished. It'll make a great article and the publicity you'll get couldn't hurt."

"That sounds wonderful," Josie said. "Doesn't that sound wonderful, Suzy?"

140

"Wonderful," I said, nodding.

"That's great," he said. "Let me check with my photographer, but this time of year he shouldn't have too much going on."

"You're far too kind, Perry," Josie said. "What did I ever do to deserve this?"

"Don't mention it," he said, studying his phone. "How's tomorrow work for you? My schedule is pretty clear."

"Tomorrow?" Josie said, glancing at me. "Tomorrow probably doesn't work, Perry. We're planning on spending the night in the city and doing some Christmas shopping tomorrow before we head home. Isn't that right, Suzy?"

"What? Oh, yeah, that's right," I said, nodding my head vigorously at Perry.

"Well, then how about the day after tomorrow?" he said. "I've heard so much about your Inn, I can't wait to see it. And I can't think of a reason to put it off until after the holidays."

"That sounds wonderful. Does that work for you, Suzy?"

"Wonderful," I said, nodding again.

"Great," he said. "I'll swing by sometime in the morning. And if you like, I'll even give you a hand taking a look at the Newfie puppy. Poor little guy."

"Even better," Josie said. "I've always wanted to get a firsthand look at you working your magic."

"Then it's a date," Perry said, getting up out of his chair.

"I can't wait," she said.

Josie pulled him close and gave him a long hug, then gently held his face with both hands and gave him a soft kiss on the lips that lingered just long enough.

I settled for a handshake.

I was lucky to get that.

Torn between wanting to get his hands on Captain and his hands all over Josie, the guy was toast.

We left him sitting behind his desk staring off into the distance and walked outside into a snowfall that was threatening to turn heavy. We climbed into the car where Jackson was sitting in the backseat flashing a huge smile.

"What are you grinning at?" Josie said.

"I've always wanted to get a firsthand look at you working your magic?" he said, laughing.

"Hey, don't start," Josie said. "And in case you didn't notice, it worked like a charm."

"Was that a little smooching I heard at the end?" Jackson said, unable to stop laughing.

"Shut up," Josie said. "I just needed to make sure the deal was closed and that he wouldn't back out."

I snorted.

"Josie, that guy will be there even if he has to walk," Jackson said.

"I would have thought you'd be thanking me," Josie snapped.

"Oh, I am," Jackson said. "You were wonderful."

"Jerk," Josie said, then looked over at me as I turned toward the highway that led south. "Where are you going? I thought we were going to have lunch in the city."

"I'm worried about the snow," I said. "I'll buy you a late lunch at the Water's Edge."

"Okay," she said. "But pull into that gas station up on the right. I'll need a snack for the ride."

"Let me guess," Jackson said, still chuckling. "Because playing a tart always makes you hungry?"

"Jackson?" Josie said.

"Yes, Josie?"

"At times like these, do you know what I like best about you?"

"No. What is it?"

"Nothing."

Chapter 23

I checked in on Sammy and Jill who were playing with all the puppies in the living room. We'd decided to bring all of them, including Captain, up to the house for the evening and I watched them chase and roll over each other then headed back into the kitchen. I sat down next to Jackson and watched Chef Claire as she headed our way carrying steaming bowls of French onion soup. She served everyone then sat down and smiled at Jeremy Tompkins, the FBI agent who was sitting across from her. Agent Tompkins had spent the afternoon installing listening devices in various sections of the Inn, and he'd proven to be both thoroughly professional and personable. As such, we'd invited him to join Jackson and Detective Abrams as our dinner guests. Since the three men arrived an hour earlier, Chef Claire had been smitten with the young agent from the FBI.

Josie and I both thought Agent Tompkins was cute, and after interacting with him we were impressed by how smart he was. But he didn't get either of our motors running, so we focused on the prospect of French onion soup, followed by beef tenderloin wrapped in a garlic-horseradish-tarragon crust. An enormous tray of roasted vegetables was in the oven, and the smell of rosemary and freshly baked bread filled the kitchen.

But Chef Claire had more on her mind than dinner, and her interactions with the Agent Tompkins had gone from a coquettish smile to overt flirting, much to the chagrin of Jackson who sat next to me brooding and staring down at his untouched bowl of soup.

"If you're not going to eat that," I whispered. "Feel free to slide it my way."

"Back off. I'm going to eat it," Jackson said, protecting his bowl with both hands. "I'm just waiting for it to cool off."

I watched Chef Claire who continued to hang on every word and laugh at everything Agent Tompkins said then looked at Jackson.

"I don't think that's going to happen, Jackson," I said.

"Suzy?"

"Yes?"

"Shut up."

Detective Abrams worked with way past the melted mozzarella and crusty bread topping into the soup. He sipped a spoonful and murmured something I couldn't hear over the racket Josie was making as her spoon rattled incessantly against the ceramic bowl.

"Hey, Miss Piggy. Take human bites," I said, laughing. "You're going to wake up the whole neighborhood."

"This is so good," Josie said, not even bothering to look up, or slow down.

"How do you like the soup, Detective Tompkins?" Chef Claire said.

"How do you like the soup, Detective Tompkins?" Jackson muttered under his breath.

Josie and I stopped eating long enough to glance at Jackson.

"Don't shoot yourself in the foot, Jackson," I whispered.

"It's incredible," Agent Tompkins said. "And please call me Jeremy."

"Oh, I'm so glad you like it, Jeremy," Chef Claire said.

"Don't make me get the hose," I whispered to Chef Claire.

"Shhh," she said, brushing her hair back from her face.

"I'd love to get the recipe if you wouldn't mind giving it to me," Agent Tompkins said.

"Not a problem at all," Chef Claire said. "Remind me to write it down for you before you leave."

"That's great. Thanks," Agent Tompkins said, glancing around the table. "I can't wait to make it for my fiancé. She's going to love it."

Crushed, Chef Claire sat back in her chair and stared down at her bowl.

"How about that, Jackson?" Josie whispered across the table. "A reprieve from the governor."

Jackson scowled at her then smiled to himself and started working on his soup.

"Are we good to go tomorrow?" I said.

"Absolutely," Detective Abrams said. "We've got listening devices installed in the reception area, the condo area, and all the exam rooms. If Dr. Long says anything the least bit incriminating, we'll get it. And we'll be there to keep a close eye on things."

"Do you really think the three of you need to be there?" I said.

All three men paused to look up from their soup and nod.

"You guys have done enough," Detective Abrams said. "And I'm still not very happy that you decided to pay Dr. Long a visit without telling me. Or that Jackson went along with it."

"You want to try stopping these two once they've made their minds up?" Jackson said.

"No, you got a point there," Detective Abrams said, shaking his head. "And I'm impressed that you figured out a way to buy more time on the fly, Josie. Telling him you wouldn't be back in town until tomorrow was a stroke of genius."

"Thanks," Josie said, barely breaking rhythm.

"She was in the zone," I said, laughing.

"And smooching," Jackson said, smiling across the table at Josie.

"Just wait, Jackson," she said. "You'll get yours."

"So, Agent Tompkins," I said. "Has the FBI confirmed who's behind the stealing of the tech secrets?"

"The FBI can't confirm or deny anything at this point. We don't comment on active cases."

"But you're here," I said, smiling at him.

"Yes," he said, wiping his mouth. "And that should tell you pretty much everything you need to know." He smiled and pushed his bowl away. "Wow. That was incredible, Chef Claire."

"I'm glad you liked it," she whispered, collecting the empty bowls.

I got up to help her and followed her to the sink.

"Are you okay?" I said to her.

"Yeah, I'm fine," she said. "I should have known better than to get my hopes up."

"Well, I know someone who's pleased by the news," I said, nodding at Jackson who was hunkered down over his soup busily catching up before the main meal was served.

Chef Claire glanced at Jackson and then removed the tenderloin from the oven. The aroma took my breath away, and I took a step backward. Chloe trotted into the kitchen and sniffed the air.

"Sorry, Chloe," I said. "It's all people food."

She barked once to show her displeasure, then rubbed herself against my leg. I picked her up and carried her back into the living room. Jill and all the puppies were worn out and napping in front of the fire except Tripod who was insisting that Sammy continue their game of fetch. I set Chloe on the floor and she and Tripod starting playing with each other.

"I can't believe how well he's doing," I said to Sammy.

"Yeah, he's amazing," Sammy said.

"You've done a great job with him, Sammy," I said.

"Thanks."

"Josie and I will give you guys a break in a bit so you can eat," I said.

"It smells amazing," Sammy said.

"Yeah," I said. "And I better get back in there before Josie gets too much of a lead."

I headed back into the kitchen and filled my plate. We ate in relative silence, pausing only to make casual chit-chat or commend Chef Claire on the food. Finally sated, I pushed my plate away and congratulated myself on the foresight I'd shown by wearing sweatpants to dinner.

Before you judge me, I need to point out that they are very stylish sweats.

"Who's ready for dessert?" Chef Claire said.

"I could eat," Josie said.

I groaned but felt compelled to ask.

"What are we having?"

"I made cannoli this afternoon," Chef Claire said.

"What kind?" Josie said.

"Like it matters," I said, laughing.

"Chocolate hazelnut," Chef Claire said.

"Oh, I love those," Josie said, giving Chef Claire a golf clap.

Chef Claire held the tray in front of Josie, and she grabbed two. The men settled for one each and then the tray stopped in front of my face. I stared at the powdered sugar-covered treats then looked up at Chef Claire.

"You're killing me."

"It's the holidays," Chef Claire said, laughing.

"So everybody keeps reminding me."

I took one of the cannoli and sighed when I bit into it.

"What time should we be here tomorrow?" Detective Abrams said.

"We open at eight, but the staff starts rolling in around half past seven," Josie said.

Detective Abrams nodded, stood, exhaled loudly.

"Chef Claire, I have to tell you that's one of the best meals I've ever had," he said.

"Me too," Agent Tompkins said, also getting up from the table.

"Thank you," Chef Claire said, glancing at Jackson who was also now standing.

"Fantastic," Jackson said, barely managing to make eye contact.

"Ladies," Detective Abrams said. "Thank you for a wonderful evening. And we will see you in the morning sometime before eight."

We waved goodbye and watched them leave. Moments later, a parade of seventeen puppies, led by Chloe strolled into the kitchen followed by Jill and Sammy.

"Evening pee time," Sammy said.

"That's adorable," Josie said, staring at the conga line of puppies crossing the kitchen floor.

"I'll take them out," I said, opening the door. "You guys better sit down and eat before Josie gets her second wind."

"Funny," Josie said, heading for the sink. "Chef Claire, grab a glass of wine and relax. Maybe you can find a movie for us. It's my turn to do dishes."

I followed the puppies outside to the snow-packed lawn. It was cold, and they didn't waste a lot of time taking care of business. Chloe herded them all back inside, and I was just about to close the door when I heard a noise coming from the Inn. I listened closely, then headed back into the kitchen.

"I think there's somebody down at the Inn," I said to Josie who was loading the dishwasher.

"Check the alarm," she said, wiping her hands on a dish towel.

I walked into the living room and noticed that the alarm had stopped working.

"That's odd," I said.

"Maybe the power's been cut," Josie said.

"You think Dr. Long decided to show up early?" I said.

"Maybe," Josie said. "But knowing Perry, my guess is that he sent his representatives."

"We need to get down there," I said.

"Yeah, we'll go in the back," she said, grabbing her coat. "You got your key?"

"Yeah," I said, pulling a hooded sweatshirt over my head. "You think we should call Jackson?" I thought about my own question before shaking my head. "On second thought, let's make sure we have a problem first. You know how Jackson is when he thinks we're getting out of control."

"Good idea," Josie said, nodding. "Chef Claire, we need a favor."

"Sure," she said.

"We might have some uninvited guests down at the Inn. We're going to head down, but if you don't hear from us in five minutes, would you call Jackson and ask him and Detective Abrams to swing by?"

"You got it," Chef Claire said, checking her watch.

"And tell them to come in quietly with no lights," I said. "They'll understand what that means."

"Okay, but be careful," Chef Claire said.

We headed out the door and down the path that led to the back of the Inn. On the back porch, we stopped to listen but heard nothing. I slid the key into the lock and slowly opened the door that led directly into the condo area where all the dogs appeared to be sleeping.

"Dark," I whispered as I slowly crept forward.

"Your powers of deduction continue to astound me," Josie whispered.

"Shhh," I whispered.

As we passed the condos, a few of the dogs stirred, and Josie and I paused long enough to let them smell and lick our hands. When they had settled back down, we slowly moved forward through the darkness. Outside the storage area where we kept dozens of fifty-pound bags of food and other items we used on a daily basis, we saw two flashlight beams in the window of the swinging door that separated the reception area from the condos.

I grabbed Josie's arm and pulled her into the cramped storage area and closed the door behind us.

"That's your plan?" Josie whispered. "Hide in the supply closet?"

"Shhh," I whispered. "I'm just buying a little time."

"That's right," Josie said. "Chef Claire will be calling Jackson in a couple of minutes."

"And you thought I didn't have a plan," I said.

"Nice try," Josie said. "Well, if we're going to be stuck in here, at least scoot over a bit. My head is jammed against a shelf."

"I can't move," I said. "It's really cramped in here."

"Hmmm. That's strange. I don't remember it being this confined," Josie deadpanned.

"What did you say?"

"Nothing," Josie whispered.

But I could tell she was stifling a laugh, and I managed to get one of my arms free and smacked her on the shoulder.

"Ow," she said. "What was that for?"

"For making that crack about my weight," I whispered.

"I didn't say a word," she whispered, then grabbed my arm. "You hear that?"

"What is that?"

"It sounds like scratching," Josie said.

"Oh, no," I said. "Did you remember to close the door on the way in?"

"I thought you did," she said.

The staccato scratching on the other side of the door continued.

"It's Chloe," I said, slowly opening the door and catching a glimpse of the two flashlights that were at the far end of the condos and heading our way. Through the dim light, I looked down at Chloe who was sitting on the floor staring up at me.

"Come here, girl."

Chloe scurried into the storage area. I closed the door and did my best to reach down and pet her. Josie groaned as I tried to make room and I gave up.

"Whoever it is must be looking for Captain," I whispered.

"Shhh," Josie said. "I can hear them talking."

"I don't see any puppies at all," the first man said. "These are all grown."

"Yeah," the second man said. "And get a look at this guy."

We heard a familiar low, guttural growl.

"Rocky," Josie whispered.

"He's huge," the first man said. "Rottweiler, right?"

"Yeah," the second man said. "Think he bites?"

"There's only one way to find out," the first man said. "Stick your hand in there."

"Yeah, right."

Rocky's growling intensified.

"They must be shining the light in his eyes," Josie whispered. "He hates that."

"Whoa," the first man said. "Look at the size of this guy."

"Tiny," I whispered.

"He's a Great Dane," the second man said. "My cousin used to have one."

"Did he bite?" the first man said.

"Nah, he was very friendly. Go ahead, pet him."

"No way," the first man said. "Let's just finish checking the rest of these cages and get out of here."

"They're not cages," I whispered. "They're condos."

"I gotta say," the first man said. "These dogs live pretty well. My bedroom at home isn't this big."

"Just wait until you get a look at the size of your prison cell," Josie whispered.

"Hey, I've got an idea," I whispered.

"What is it?"

"No, never mind," I whispered. "It might put Chloe in danger."

"Suzy, I doubt if they have plans to shoot any dogs," Josie whispered. "They're here to steal one."

"I guess you're right," I said. "Okay, who knows if it will work, but it might be worth a shot."

I reached down and was finally able to get my hand on the top of Chloe's head.

"Chloe, green button. Green button, girl."

"Suzy, you were just finally able to get her to stop pushing it. Now you're telling her it's okay? You're going to confuse her."

"Shhh," I said. "Green button, Chloe. Go get the green button."

I slowly opened the door partway, and Chloe scurried out of the storage area. The green button was the one that automatically opened all of the condo's inside doors. Chloe had become enamored with it as soon as she figured out that, with a push of a button, all the dogs could get together and play. At first, we thought it was funny and cute. After a week we decided that having to herd all the dogs back into their condos several times a day wasn't cute but downright annoying. I'd worked with Chloe to eliminate the behavior and had finally gotten her trained. Now I was giving her permission to do it again. I doubted that she would understand that this was a one-time exception to the rule, but she was the smartest dog I'd ever seen, so anything was possible.

"Nah, there's no puppies here," the first man said. "I think Perry has got his wires crossed."

We heard the soft whirring sound and I peered through a small slit in the door.

"What a smart dog," I whispered with pride.

"Hey, George," the first man said.

"Yeah?"

"What's that standing behind you?"

"Huh? Uh-oh."

"Is that a Rottweiler?"

"Yup. Don't look now, but I think there's one standing behind you, too."

"Uh-oh. Nice doggy."

Then their screams filled the condo area. We heard the sound of both flashlights clattering to the floor. We burst out of the storage area, and I scrambled for the light switch, and the room was bathed in light. The men were on the floor desperately trying to escape the clutches of Rocky and Bullwinkle, a pair of Rottweilers from the same litter we'd had since they were puppies. Very gentle by nature, but extremely protective of their territory and both of us, each dog had one of the men's ankles in a death grip.

Both men stopped screaming when they saw us staring down at them.

"Get him off me," the first man said.

"Now why would I do that?" Josie said.

"Oooh, good question," I said, laughing.

"I'm warning you, lady," the first man said.

"You're not very bright, are you?" Josie said, shaking her head. "Get him Bullwinkle."

The Rottweiler tightened his grip on the man's ankle and shook his leg like a chew toy. Another round of screams filled the condo area.

"Okay, Bullwinkle," Josie said, laughing. "Easy does it."

Bullwinkle paused to reposition his grip on the ankle and emitted a deep growl that made the hair on the back of my neck stand up. I could only imagine the physiological effects the man writing in pain on the floor was experiencing.

"Let's put them in one of the condos," I said.

"Good idea," Josie said, then looked down at the two immobilized, terror-stricken men. "You want to crawl in, or would you like Rocky and Bullwinkle to drag you?"

"Okay, lady," the first man said. "You win."

"Rocky. Bullwinkle," Josie said. "Let go."

Both dogs released their grip but remained sitting and growling inches away. The second man dragged himself into a nearby condo, and Bullwinkle trotted in after him and sat down blocking the doorway. The first man made a different, and rather poor, choice. As soon as Rocky released his ankle, he scrambled to his feet and made a hobbled beeline for the exit.

Josie glanced at me, shaking her head.

"He must be a slow learner. Okay, genius, have it your way," she said, doing her best not to laugh. "Go get him, Rocky,"

The Rottweiler tore after the man, leaped through the air, and grabbed the back of his thigh. The man dropped like a rock and screamed again as blood began to ooze onto the floor. Rocky must have enjoyed the taste because he repositioned his mouth and went back for seconds. Then the dog began dragging him toward the condo where his partner was cowering against the back wall. The man managed to crawl inside, and Rocky let go upon Josie's command.

"I'm bleeding," the first man said, wincing as he examined his leg.

"Yes, I noticed," Josie said. "You're going to need stitches."

"I am?"

"Yeah. A lot of them," she said.

"How do you know that?"

"Because I'm a vet and I know a deep puncture wound when I see it," she said.

"If you're a vet, then you know how to do stitches, right?"

"Absolutely," Josie said.

"Well, don't just stand there, sew me up," the man said.

"Trust me, sweetie," Josie said, glaring at him. "The last thing you want right now is me anywhere near you with a sharp object in my hand."

I grabbed a stack of towels from the storage area and tossed them inside the condo.

"Wrap them tight," I said.

Chloe trotted over, and I bent down to rub her head.

"What a good girl," I said.

"That dog is scary smart," Josie said.

"She certainly is. Now watch this," I said. "Chloe. Red button."

We watched as Chloe trotted over to the panel near the entrance. She hopped up on the stool, stood on her back legs, and used a front paw to press the button. We heard the soft whirring sound again as the condo doors slowly closed. Just for the fun of it, we left Rocky and Bullwinkle in the condo with our two uninvited guests.

Seconds later, Jackson and Detective Abrams appeared in the doorway with guns drawn. They took a look around and saw the trail of blood on the floor.

"Are you guys okay?" Jackson said.

"We're fine," I said. "But I think those two might need some help."

"Let me guess," Detective Abrams said, glancing at the two men. "Dr. Long didn't feel like waiting until tomorrow."

"Yeah, so he sent these two geniuses," Josie said.

"What happened to them?" Jackson said.

"Rocky and Bullwinkle had a late night snack," I said.

"Rottweiler bite, huh?" Detective Abrams said.

"Yeah."

"Good," Detective Abrams said, heading for the condo where the two men continued to cower against the back wall. "You mind leaving the dogs in there while I have a little chat with our friends?"

"Nothing would make us happier," Josie said, grabbing a mop from the storage area.

"Let me take care of that," I said, taking the mop from her hand.

"Are you sure?"

"Yeah. Why don't you head up to the house and grab yourself a snack? I know how hungry adrenaline always makes you."

"I could eat."

Chapter 24

We decided to have Sammy and Jill stay up at the house with the puppies while Josie and I dealt with Dr. Perry Long. A little after seven we headed down to the Inn and said good morning to all the dogs, paying extra attention to Rocky and Bullwinkle for their efforts last night. Josie got Captain comfortable in his own condo near the middle of the room, and we reclosed all the doors and made sure that Chloe was with us when we returned to my office to wait. It wouldn't be a good time for her to starting pushing buttons.

We heard a car pull into the parking lot, and I glanced through the window and saw Jackson, Detective Abrams, and Agent Tompkins climb out of a non-descript sedan and head our way. They joined us in the office, and Josie tossed each of them a pair of the dark blue scrubs all our staff wore at work.

"You really expect me to wear these?" Jackson said, turning the scrubs over in his hands.

"You bet we do," Josie said, chuckling. "And by the time this is over, you'll be thanking me."

"I don't think I like the sound of this," Jackson said. "What do you expect me to do?"

"Nothing that a Junior Technician wouldn't do on a daily basis," Josie said, flashing a smile at me.

I rolled my desk chair back to reveal a large plastic garbage can on wheels lined with a trash bag. Two long objects sat inside in garbage can. I held both objects up and showed them to Jackson.

"Your shovel and your custom made scooper," I said. "You have two acres to cover so I suggest you change clothes and get busy."

Detective Abrams and Agent Tompkins tried, but were unable to suppress their laughter.

"Let me get this straight," Jackson said. "You expect me to clean up after your dogs?"

"Absolutely," Josie said. "What did you think you were going to be doing?"

"Well, when you mentioned that we would be playing the role of one of your staff, I just assumed that I'd be one of the vets working here. Or at least a vet assistant."

"Sorry, Jackson," I deadpanned. "But you're not qualified."

"Qualified to do what?" Jackson said. "Pretend to be someone I'm not?"

"Yeah, you got a point there," I said, nodding. "But we're sorry, you're on clean-up today." I gestured toward the two-acre area that sat directly outside the warm office. "Your poo-pile awaits."

"I can't believe you two," Jackson said, heading for the door, scrubs in hand.

"Relax, Jackson," Josie said, beaming at him. "It's winter. And that makes your job so much easier."

"Does it now?" Jackson said, glaring at Josie.

"Sure. Scooping is so much easier when everything is frozen."

Jackson turned and started for the door but stopped when I cleared my throat.

"Don't forget these," I said, rolling the garbage can across the office. "When you're done, just remove and tie the plastic bag and toss it in the big bin in back. Then put in a fresh bag and wash the shovel and scooper and put them back in the garbage can."

"Yes, your Majesty," he said.

Jackson tossed the scrubs over his shoulder and grabbed the handle on the can. He pushed it toward the door grumbling as he left the office and all the way down the hall.

"That was fun," Josie said.

"What about us?" Detective Abrams said.

"We thought we'd put you in the condo area. All you need to do is keep an eye on the dogs. Feel free to play with them, make sure they have water, stuff like that," I said.

"And if Perry so much as lays a finger on Captain, feel free to shoot him," Josie said.

"Or maybe just break his arm," I said.

"Yeah," Josie said, glancing at Detective Abrams. "That would be your decision."

"Thanks," Detective Abrams deadpanned. "I appreciate you trusting me to make the right call."

"You're pretty funny for a cop, Detective Abrams," Josie said, laughing.

"Agent Tompkins, we thought you would probably want to handle reception. You'll be able to monitor our conversations, and I doubt if we'll get any walk-ins this morning."

"Sounds great," Agent Tompkins said. "Would you mind showing me how your phone system works? As your receptionist, I should probably know how to transfer a call."

"Good catch," Josie said, getting up off the couch. "Come on, I'll walk you through it.

They left the office, and Detective Abrams got up from his chair.

"Where can I get changed?"

"Out the office to the right," I said.

"Should I meet you in the condo area?"

"Sure," I said. "And thanks for doing this, Detective Abrams."

"It's what they pay me to do," he said, shrugging. "And besides, I never get a chance to hang out with dogs all day and get paid for it."

"You should give it a try," I said. "It's not a bad way to go through life."

"Yeah, I'm sure you're right about that," he said, giving me a small wave as he left.

I paced back and forth for a few minutes, then decided there were better ways for me to spend my time. I headed for reception and waited for Josie to finish with Agent Tompkins. Then we headed to the condos and found Detective Abrams in Tiny's condo. The Great Dane had the detective on his back and was using his front paws to pin the detective's shoulders to the floor. Detective Abrams was laughing as he struggled to get loose.

"I think he has you beat," I said.

"This guy is great," Detective Abrams said, climbing to his feet. "Is he available for adoption?"

"No, we're sorry," Josie said, shaking her head. "But Tiny's not going anywhere."

"Too bad," Detective Abrams said.

"But we should have a litter of German Shepherds available in a couple of months," I said. "And I think we still have one of the Labs."

"Nope," Josie said. "Sammy said she was adopted yesterday."

"Really? Who got her?"

"The Andersons."

"Perfect. They're a great family," I said, then stopped when I heard a car.

I glanced out the window at the play area. Jackson, scooper in hand, was looking toward the front of the Inn, then he turned around and saw me. He gave me a quick thumbs-up, then went back to work.

"He's here," I said.

"Let's go through it again," Josie said.

"Okay, remember to keep it simple," Detective Abrams said. "Let him take all the photos he wants, then give him the tour. At some point, he's going to want to take a look at the Newfie. Take the puppy to the exam room right off the reception area. Josie, I'll go in with you as your assistant. And Jackson and Agent Tompkins will be standing guard right outside the exam room as well as the back door that leads to the condo area. Dr. Long's not going anywhere."

"What if he gets violent or starts making threats?" Josie said.

"If he does, just do your best to stay calm and quiet and leave him to me," Detective Abrams said.

"Okay," Josie said. "But if he does anything to hurt Captain, I'm not making any promises."

A buzzer sounded that indicated someone wanted to see us in reception, so Josie and I headed that way. Detective Abrams picked up a broom and did his best to look busy. Josie and I stepped into reception and found Dr. Perry Long regaling Agent Tompkins with a story about himself. A woman was glancing around the reception area with her back to us.

"Josie," Dr. Long said when he heard us. "Hello, Suzy."

"Perry," Josie gushed as she moved in for a hug. "You made it."

"I wouldn't have missed it for the world," he said. "Josie and Suzy, I'd like you to meet Cynthia Chambers, photographer extraordinaire."

"Oh, Perry," the woman said, turning around to face us. "You're such a flatterer."

She smiled at us and extended her hand. I did my best to hide my surprise and glanced at Josie who appeared to be doing the same. Standing before us was Gloria Fullerton, renowned technology consultant and ex-wife of Tom, sister to the deceased Jerome, Perry's girlfriend, and, if the photos weren't lying, quite the avid golfer.

"Nice to meet you," I said, shaking her hand.

"What a beautiful place you have here," the woman calling herself Cynthia said.

"Hi, Cynthia," Josie said. "Thanks."

"Hello, Josie. Perry has told me all about your prowess as a vet."

"Well, I wouldn't put too much stock in that," Josie said, smiling. "I hear he's a drinker."

They both roared with laughter.

"Didn't I tell you she was funny?" Perry said.

"Yes, you did, Perry," she said. "You certainly did."

I exhaled loudly and snuck a glance at Agent Tompkins who also seemed tired of the sugary chit-chat.

"What do you say we get started?" Josie said.

"Perfect," Perry said. "How about we get the photos out of the way and then we can take a look at that gorgeous Newfie puppy?"

"Perfect," Josie said, beaming at both of them.

We headed out the front door and walked along the side of the Inn until we reached the back area. As we walked, Josie rambled on about the Inn and our expansion plans. Perry and Cynthia nodded, and she snapped several photos along the way. When we reached the spot where the expansion would extend off from the main building we stopped, and Josie and I spent a few minutes explaining what our plans were. This was the easy part since everything we told them was consistent with what we would be doing as soon as Spring arrived.

Jackson wandered over dragging the garbage can behind him.

"Okay, I'm done out here," Jackson said.

"That's great, Jackson," I said, glancing around the play area. "It looks like you missed a couple, but you can take care of those on your afternoon rounds."

"Sure, Suzy," he said, giving me the evil eye. "I'll be happy to."

"I'd like you to meet Jackson," Josie said. "He's one of our newest junior technicians."

"Dr. Perry Long," he said, extending his hand toward Jackson. "And this is my photographer, Cynthia."

"Nice to meet you," Jackson said.

"You look like a man who loves his job," Perry said.

"Actually, I do love my job," Jackson said, nodding.

"That's great. And don't worry about starting out in a low-level position. A lot of people in this industry started out at the bottom and worked their way up."

"Did you?" Jackson said.

"Oh, no. Of course not," Perry said, laughing. "But hang in there, Jackson. Even Rod Stewart started out as a gravedigger."

"Good for Rod," Jackson whispered, giving me the evil eye.

"If you've got all the photos you need, Cynthia, why don't we head inside where it's warm?" I said, glancing at Jackson and rolling my eyes at him.

We entered the condo area and were greeted by a round of happy barks and yips.

"Well, somebody is sure glad to see you," Perry said, glancing down the long line of condos. "These are nice accommodations. Well done, ladies. I'm impressed."

"Thanks," Josie said. "We like to think so."

"Make sure you get some good shots of this area, Cynthia," Perry said.

He strolled past the condos until he stopped in front of Captain's condo. The puppy was rolling around on the floor and pawing at his face. He stopped when he noticed us watching and trotted toward the gated entrance and wagged his tail. Perry leaned down and rubbed Captain's head.

"He's gorgeous," Perry said, glancing over his shoulder at Josie. "Should we go take a look at him?"

"Sure, Perry," she said, unlatching the door to the condo.

Captain climbed up into her arms, and she held him close to her chest. She turned and headed for the door that led back into reception.

"Let's take him into exam room one," Josie said. "Joe, can you give me a hand while we examine Captain?"

"Sure, Doc," Detective Abrams said, then leaned his broom against the wall and headed our way.

"Since we're both vets, Josie, I don't think we'll need a tech, will we?" Perry said, obviously not happy about having another person in the exam room.

"I never do anything like this without Joe in the room," Josie said, casually. "He's like another pair of eyes for me. I'm sure you understand."

"Sure, I get it. I have my favorite techs I always like to work with. Lead the way," Perry said. "Cynthia, why don't you stay here with Suzy and get some more photos and background information on the Inn?"

I looked at Jackson who was staring back at me. We hadn't discussed how we were going to handle the photographer while Josie and Detective Abrams dealt with Perry. I couldn't believe we'd forgotten to talk about it.

I guess I could put the onus on myself for the oversight, but I decided to blame the three cops. After all, they did this stuff for a living; I was just a part-timer.

"What would you like to see next, Cynthia?" I said.

"Well, I'm not sure," she said. "I think I've got all the photos I need, and I have to admit that I'm not much of a dog lover."

"Really?" I said, frowning.

"Truth be told, I'm afraid of them," she said, glancing around nervously at the condos.

"Then you must meet Rocky and Bullwinkle," I said.

"What?"

"Nothing," I said. "Let me show you our automatic water system. It's how we keep all the water bowls full without having to worry about doing it manually."

"It sounds lovely," she said, following me.

"So is this your full-time job, Cynthia?" I said.

"Pretty much," she said, glancing around.

"Do you have any hobbies?" I said, glancing at Jackson who was trailing about ten feet behind us.

"Oh, I like dabbling with computers and technology," she said.

"Interesting," I said.

"And I play a lot of golf," she said. "It's a real passion of mine."

"I never got into golf," I said. "It looks like it takes a lot of time to get good at it."

"Oh, it does," she said. "But when you love something, all that time seems well spent."

"Oh, I agree completely," I said. "So what do you usually shoot, Gloria?"

The woman who was going by the name Cynthia stopped and stared at me.

"What did you say?"

"Oops," I said.

Her eyes widened, and the woman no longer going by the name Cynthia started to turn around. She opened her mouth as if preparing to call out a warning when Jackson came up behind her, draped a hand over her mouth and pulled her hands back and snapped on a pair of handcuffs with the other. His moves looked like a cop version of a choreographed dance routine.

I would spend the next several days replaying those few seconds in my head, and I still don't know how he did it.

"Okay, Gloria," Jackson said. "Here's what's going to happen next. You're going to spend some time with Rocky and Bullwinkle in their condo."

Gloria's eyes widened even further.

"And as long as you sit quietly and don't say a word, those gorgeous Rottweilers won't do anything to hurt you," I said, opening the door to the condo.

"But if you do anything stupid, like the two gentlemen you sent here last night did, Rocky and Bullwinkle will be more than happy to do whatever Suzy tells them to. Do you understand?"

Gloria nodded, and Jackson walked her into the condo. She sat down cowering with her back against the wall glancing back and forth at the two dogs who were sitting a few feet away staring at her with a soft throaty growl and the perfect amount of frothy drool hanging from their jowls.

"I didn't send those two guys," Gloria said, unable to take her eyes of the Rottweilers. "I mean I didn't send any guys here."

"Hold that thought for a moment, Gloria," I said. "I'll be right back."

"Where are you going?" Jackson said.

"I think I should get Joe out here," I said, winking at Jackson. "I need to duck out, and I'm not sure you'll be able to control Rocky and Bullwinkle all by yourself."

"What?" Gloria said, glancing up at us. "What did you say?"

"Relax, Gloria," I said. "I just want to make sure the dogs behave themselves when you start talking. And if you're as smart as your ex-husband says you are, you will start talking."

"Suzy, please don't do anything stupid," Jackson said.

"I'll do my best, Jackson," I said, punching him on the arm.

I headed into reception and nodded at Agent Tompkins who was standing outside the exam room. I knocked softly before entering.

Josie, Perry, and Detective Abrams glanced up from the puppy that was on the exam table.

"Sorry to interrupt, but you have a call, Joe. It's your wife, and she sounds pretty upset. You can take it on the phone in the condo area. I think she really wants to talk."

Detective Abrams nodded at me, then smiled and went out through the back door of the exam room. Josie glanced at me, and I gave her a slight nod to continue.

"I hope she's okay," Josie said.

"I think she'll be fine," I said, looking at Perry. "She's seven months pregnant."

"Really?" Perry said. "Joe looks like he's in his fifties."

"Second marriage. You know how that works," I said.

"More than I care to admit," Perry said, laughing.

Josie and I forced ourselves to laugh along. Then Perry refocused on the puppy.

"I don't know, Josie," he said, rubbing the back of Captain's neck. "I'm not feeling anything except what appears to be a small scab."

"You know, Perry, that's exactly what I thought. I don't know how he could have gotten it."

"Hmmm," Perry said as he continued to gently rub his fingers along the dog's back.

"You don't think someone was cutting on him, do you?" Josie said.

"I sure hope not," Perry said, staring off into space. "That would be bad." Then he remembered where he was and who he was talking to. "I mean, what sort of person would do something like that?"

"You know, Perry. I've been asking myself the same question," Josie said.

Detective Abrams reentered the exam room.

"Is everything okay?" I said.

"Yes, everything is just fine," Detective Abrams said, smiling at me. "She just needs to get a few things off her chest."

"I hope you gave her enough time to talk," I said, smiling back at him.

"I certainly did," Detective Abrams said. "Actually, she's still going strong. I just came back in to do one more thing before I go back to hear the rest of it."

"What's that?" I said.

"Watch closely," Detective Abrams said as he reached behind his back to grab the gun tucked inside his scrubs. He pointed it at Perry's face.

"Are you out of your mind?" Perry stared at the gun, then looked at Josie. "Why is your tech pointing a gun at me, Josie?"

"I guess that's a reasonable question," Josie said, shrugging. "Detective Abrams, why are you pointing your gun at him?"

"Because Dr. Long is under arrest."

"That's preposterous," Perry said. "What on earth are you talking about?"

"Save it, Perry," Detective Abrams said. "Gloria is out there singing like a canary and trying to cut a deal for herself."

At the mention of Gloria's name, Perry's shoulders sagged, and he staggered backward into a chair and sat down staring at the floor.

Detective Abrams glanced at the front door of the exam room.

"Okay, Jeremy. C'mon in."

Agent Tompkins, gun drawn, entered.

"Are we good?" he said.

"Oh, we're better than good," Detective Abrams said. "Dr. Long, I'd like you to meet Agent Tompkins from the FBI."

"What?" Perry said. "You're with the FBI?"

"Yeah," he said. "But I do have to say that this dog thing is pretty cool."

"And to think that I shared my recipe for red clam chowder with you," Perry said.

"Yeah, thanks again for that," Agent Tompkins said, returning his gun to its holster. "I think my fiancé is going to love it."

"Red clam chowder?" Josie said. "That sounds yummy."

"Ugh," I said.

If you remember, I hate all things fishy with a passion.

Josie cradled Captain in her arms, and the puppy licked her face. Josie laughed and snuggled the dog tight.

"You found the chip, didn't you?" Perry said.

"Yup," Josie said.

"How on earth did you do that?" he said.

"Does it matter?" Josie said.

"No, probably not," Perry said.

"Perry, why would you do something this stupid?" Josie said.

"Mostly for the money," he said, shrugging. "And Gloria can be very persuasive when she wants to be."

"Yeah, well, unfortunately for her, so can Rocky and Bullwinkle," I said, then looked at Detective Abrams. "Are we done here?"

"Yeah, for now," he said. "We'll probably need to talk later to tie up some loose ends, but you and Josie can get out of here. Thanks for all your help. Great job."

"Just let us know when you're done so we can lock up. I think we'll take the rest of the day off."

"Oooh, good call," Josie said. "Pizza, wine and a WIJ?"

"Perfect," I said. "I think Chef Claire has the day off. Let's ask her to see if she wants to join us."

"Sure," Josie said. "But that means we'll need to order two extra-large pies."

"Good call. I want pepperoni and mushroom on one," I said.

"That sounds good," Josie said. "I'm thinking sausage and onion on the other."

"I'm in," I said.

"And anchovies," Josie deadpanned.

"Do it, and you're dead," I said.

"They don't taste that fishy when they're on a pizza," Josie said.

"No."

"Fine. I'll get them on the side," Josie said. "But they're just not as good that way."

"Anchovies on a pizza," I said, shaking my head. "You should be ashamed of yourself."

"Are they always like this?" Perry said, bewildered by our conversation.

"This is nothing," Detective Abrams said, holding Dr. Long's hands behind his back and snapping on a pair of handcuffs. "You should see them argue over who gets the last slice."

Josie and I headed for the house, and I ordered the pizzas as we walked up the path.

"About forty-five minutes," I said, putting my phone back in my pocket.

"That long?" Josie said, wrapping her arms around herself for warmth.

"I think you'll make it," I said, laughing.

"Maybe. We did good," Josie said, gently punching my arm.

"Yeah," I said, nodding. "About the only thing we didn't do was figure out who shot Jerome."

"I still think the Baxter Brothers had something to do with it," Josie said.

I thought about it, then shook my head.

"No, I don't think so," I said. "If they had, they would have been long gone by now. As strange as this might sound, I don't see a connection between the puppy mill and Jerome's murder."

"You really think it was just a coincidence that he got shot at the same time he was calling us about the puppies he left on our doorstep?"

"Yeah, I do."

"Well, if that's the case, and there isn't any connection, then we're completely missing something."

"It wouldn't be the first time," I said, laughing.

I reached the verandah and was about to go inside the house when a lightbulb went off in my head. I stood on the porch and stared off into the distance, deep in thought.

"What is it?" Josie said.

I walked inside, removed my coat, and bent down to say hello to Chloe. Then I sat down on the couch and stared into the fireplace.

"Are you going to tell me what's going on?" Josie said, picking Captain up before plopping down in one of the overstuffed chairs.

172

"It's probably nothing," I said. "But remind me to call Detective Abrams in the morning."

Chapter 25

Two days before Christmas, we had our annual dinner at the house for what we called our inner circle. Chef Claire prepared an Italian feast that started with a duck sausage and mushroom soup with polenta dumplings that was a total knee buckler and was followed by a squash risotto, then a creamy chicken asparagus fettuccine. After that, Chef Claire served a baked fish concoction that was surrounded by roasted tomatoes and onions bathing in a red wine sauce. I had to admit that it smelled fantastic but skipped the course and temporarily adjourned to the living room to play with the dogs.

Chloe and Captain had already become fast friends, and they were rolling around on the floor with Wally, Detective Abrams's basset hound and Jackson's bulldog, Sluggo. Tripod sat on my lap watching the scene play out in front of him. Josie had removed the last bandage from his leg earlier in the day, and he was finally ready to transition into his three-legged journey of what I hoped would be a long, healthy life. Finally, the dogs wore themselves out, and all five fell asleep in front of the fire.

"Okay, it's safe to come back now," Josie said, laughing in the doorway.

I got up and went back to the dining room where Chef Claire was passing around a tray that contained a garlic beef roast. I filled my plate with slices of the roast and generous samples of every side dish within reach and started working.

"I still don't know how you figured out that Fullerton was the one who shot Jerome," Detective Abrams said.

I swallowed and wiped my face with a napkin, then gently set my knife and fork down on the side of my plate. I took a ladylike sip of water, then glanced at my mother who nodded in approval at my improved table manners.

Maybe I could pull this off when the situation called for it.

"It started with a simple what-if question I asked myself. If the murderer wasn't anyone connected to what was going on with the dogs, who was left? And then it came to me when you mentioned something that Gloria told you," I said, reaching for my wine glass. "She said that she hadn't spoken with Jerome since he left Albany and didn't know how to reach him. And that was just fine with Gloria because she didn't want anything to do with her brother."

"No, she didn't," Detective Abrams said. "At least she didn't after she caught Jerome trying to sell one of the implanted chips. That's why our working theory was that she was the one who shot him. But her alibi turned out to be air tight."

"Where was she when Jerome got shot anyway?" Josie said, pausing to catch her breath.

"She was playing golf with Perry at Pebble Beach," Detective Abrams said.

For some reason, Josie and I found that bit of news particularly funny. We laughed until we started to get strange looks from everyone else around the table.

"Yes," I said, composing myself. "After Josie and I talked to Fullerton at his office in Albany, we were convinced that Gloria had to be the one who was paying for Jerome's cellphone. Fullerton's acting skills were pretty impressive."

"So this man Fullerton was the one paying for the phone all along?" my mother said, reaching for a plate of roasted red peppers.

"Yeah, and he confirmed that this morning when we arrested him," Detective Abrams. "Suzy was the one who put it together."

"That's my girl," my mother said, beaming.

"Thanks, Mom," I said. "Gloria said that she forced Fullerton to fire Jerome when she caught him trying to sell one of the chips that were implanted in the puppies. After I heard that, I knew that Fullerton's story about how Jerome had been selling the access codes of his customers was a total lie."

"Why would he lie about that?" my mother said.

"To protect his ex-wife," I said. "It was obvious when we met with Fullerton that he still loved Gloria. He kept singing her praises, and he couldn't even take the photos of the two of them off his office wall."

"So he was hoping to reconcile with her?" my mother said.

"Yeah," I said. "Go figure."

"Silly man," my mother said.

"And when Detective Abrams mentioned that Gloria had told the FBI that Fullerton had always blamed Jerome for the problems in their marriage, the lightbulb went off in my head. Apparently, Jerome was always telling Gloria that she could do better and that Fullerton was a total loser."

"Well, if anybody would know a loser when he saw one, it would be Jerome," Jackson said.

"But Jerome did call us and save a lot of dogs in the process," I said.

"Yeah, I guess he did," Jackson said, nodding. "I'll give him that."

"I still don't understand where Jerome's phone fits into all this," my mother said.

"Fullerton basically hinted, without actually coming out and saying it, that Gloria had kept Jerome's phone active so that she could stay in contact with him. But after she told Detective Abrams that she didn't want anything to do with him, I knew that Fullerton had to be the one who'd kept the phone active the whole time."

"You know, Suzy," Detective Abrams said. "It is okay for you to call me Joe."

"Nah," I said, shaking my head. "It just doesn't seem right."

Josie snorted, and Detective Abrams' wife laughed.

"Maybe I'll try that," his wife said.

"That's okay, dear," Detective Abrams said, laughing. "Just keep calling me sir, and we'll be fine."

"In your dreams," she said, kissing him on the cheek.

"So this guy Fullerton wanted the phone active so he could keep tabs on Jerome?" my mother said.

"Yes. Keep tabs on Jerome and then take him out when the time was right," Detective Abrams said. "It took Fullerton a while to start talking this morning, but after we hinted his testimony might help his wife get a reduced sentence, he blabbed for an hour."

"Will it?" Josie said.

"What? Get her a reduced sentence?" Detective Abrams said.

"Yeah."

"Not a chance," he said, shaking his head.

"Pretty sneaky, Detective Abrams," Josie said, grinning at him.

"Hey, I said it was a hint, not a promise," he said, shrugging. "Gloria's going away for a very long time."

"What were they smuggling on those computer chips?" Josie said.

"The better question is what weren't they smuggling," Detective Abrams said. "With her reputation as a tech expert, her consulting work put her deep inside a lot of companies."

"And she was selling it to Perry's buddies on the Canadian side?" Josie said.

"Yeah, between Perry's clients and the Happy Family Time stores, they had quite the little network going on," he said. "And since a lot of the stuff they were selling was emerging, cutting-edge technology, it's going to be hard to prove copyright infringement. You know, who's to say who invented what and when? It's a mess."

"Is Perry talking?" I said.

"Oh, yeah. My buddies in Ottawa tell me that Perry is doing everything he can to save his own skin."

"Everybody's talking," Jackson said. "I like it when that happens."

"Yeah, it does make our job a bit easier, doesn't it?" Detective Abrams said, allowing himself a rare chuckle.

"So where did the smuggled dogs come from?" Josie said.

"Gloria was working with a breeder in Albany," Detective Abrams said. "They were one of the first people she gave up. Agent Tompkins and a couple of his colleagues paid them a little visit yesterday."

"Good," Josie said, attacking a slice of beef.

"So how does that despicable pair of brothers fit into this whole thing?" my mother said, taking a sip of wine.

"We think it was Jerome who recruited the Baxter Brothers to smuggle the dogs across the border. And when they learned from Jerome about how the dogs were being used they decided that starting up a puppy mill would be a piece of cake," I said, then kicked myself under the table and glanced at Josie.

"Maybe later," Josie said, shaking her head. "I'm full at the moment."

"What a couple of geniuses," Detective Abrams said.

"Where did they get the dogs to start the puppy mill?" my mother said.

"The Baxter Brothers were following advertisements for upcoming litters of various breeds and then stealing the pregnant dogs," Josie said.

"That's disgusting," my mother said, shaking her head.

"Yeah, it's the worst," I said. "But Josie and I have managed to track down the owners of the three adult females. And all the owners have agreed not to make any claim on the three litters. Which is a good thing, since all the puppies have already been adopted."

"And they all agreed just like that?" my mother said.

"They did as soon as I mentioned dog smuggling and puppy mill in the same sentence," Josie said, smiling. "But they're happy to get their family dogs back, so everybody wins."

"Are you keeping an eye on the Baxter Brothers, Jackson?" I said.

"I've been trying," he said. "But they've disappeared. I swung by Rooster's place yesterday, and their boat is gone."

"That's too bad," Josie said. "I'd love to have a little chat with them."

"I'm not sure that's going to be possible," Jackson said. "After I noticed that their boat was gone, I asked Rooster about it, and he said the Baxter boys had left a few days earlier."

"And?" Josie said.

"And when I asked him if he knew where they went, Rooster got the strangest smile on his face and said he wasn't sure where they ended up, but he was pretty sure they'd sunk to a new low."

He glanced around the table to make sure everyone had time to digest what he'd just told us.

"Wow," Josie said. "Are you going to investigate?"

"Why on earth would I do that?" Jackson said. "For all I know, the Baxter Brothers are spending the winter in Florida."

We heard a knock on the kitchen door and then a familiar voice.

"We're in the dining room, Freddie," I said.

Freddie, our local medical examiner, entered and sat down in the empty chair next to Chef Claire. It was obvious that they had patched up their recent disagreement. I glanced at Jackson who also noticed their friendly greeting. He frowned and pushed his plate away.

I caught Josie staring at what was left on the plate, waited until I caught her eye, then shook my head. She made a face at me but left Jackson's plate alone. She settled for another slice of beef from the serving tray. She made another face at me, then smiled, and started working.

"Sorry I'm late," Freddie said, filling his plate. "I was doing some Christmas shopping and then got caught in a storm on the drive back. If it keeps moving our way, we're in for at least a foot."

We all groaned.

"But at least we'll have a white Christmas," Freddie said, beaming at Chef Claire.

"My first one," Chef Claire said.

"Enjoy it," Josie said. "The second and third don't quite measure up."

"You're such a Scrooge," I said, laughing.

"Actually, I prefer the term realist."

Chapter 26

"Are you sure you don't want to be Santa?"

"No, I don't think I can fill that suit out."

"Are you taking a shot at my weight?"

"Not at all," Josie deadpanned. "You just have broader... shoulders."

"Funny," I said, staring down at the red suit and black boots spread out on the couch.

"I'm not sure about these," Josie said, staring at the odd looking pair of shoes she was holding.

"Hey, I'm going to be wearing that," I snapped, pointing at the suit. "And since I am, you're wearing the elf shoes."

"Well, excuse me," she said, laughing. "Who's the Scrooge now? Besides, wasn't this your idea in the first place?"

"No, all I said was that it would be fun to deliver the puppies on Christmas Eve. You're the one who came up with the idea to go as Santa and one of his elves."

"Relax, Santa. You're supposed to be jolly," Josie said, patting my stomach. "And you should probably start practicing your ho-ho-hos."

As cranky as I was trying to sound, I was actually very excited about what we'd named, Operation Christmas Eve. Several people had already stopped by the Inn and picked up their dogs. But twelve families, most of them with young children, were as excited as both of us about the prospect of delivering a dozen puppies to their new homes. More specifically, we were excited to see the looks on the faces of the kids who were getting a puppy for Christmas.

I wrapped a couple of large pillows around my stomach and pulled the red suit on. I looked at myself in the mirror, examined myself from several angles, and decided I looked like a pregnant bagel dog. Then I spent several minutes trying to get the white eyebrows and beard right, then slid the floppy red hat over my head. When I decided I could probably pull it off, I waddled into the living room and had Josie help me get the long black boots on.

Josie was wearing a long green jacket over a yellow bodysuit and a pair of shoes with toes that curled back. Her hat was green and yellow and way too big for her head.

"Don't say a word," she warned as she took a few tentative steps. "I know I'm going to wipe out in these shoes."

"Just don't do it when you're holding one of the puppies," I said.

"Yeah, thanks. I'll try to remember that," she said. "And feel free to shoot me the next time I get an idea like this."

"Don't worry," I said, waddling toward the kitchen door. "It's already on my to-do list."

Chef Claire looked up from the pot of soup she was stirring on the stove and choked back a laugh.

"Oh, don't you two look adorable?" Chef Claire said, grabbing her phone and snapping a picture before we could stop her. "I think this would look great framed and hanging in the restaurant. Maybe we'll put it in the bar above the fireplace."

"How about in the fireplace?" Josie said. "Okay, we're out of here."

"Have fun," Chef Claire said. "This will be ready by the time you get back."

"What is it?" Josie said, glancing inside the large pot.

"It's a new gumbo recipe I came up with," Chef Claire said. "I was going to just make soup from the leftovers we had from the other night, but they seem to have disappeared."

182

"Yeah, sorry about that," Josie said, tiptoeing her way to the door. "Man, I don't know how the elves do it. These shoes are brutal."

We slowly worked our way down the steps holding onto each other for balance and found Jill sitting in the backseat of the car that was already running. She was doing her best to babysit all the puppies that were in two large boxes. Josie and I spent a few minutes petting them and then settled into our seats.

"Thanks for doing this, Jill," I said. "It won't take too long."

"I wouldn't miss this for the world, Santa," she said, laughing.

"Don't start," I said, backing out of the driveway. "Who's up first?"

"The Williamson family," Josie said. "One of the Cockers. Wilber. Good name."

"Here you go," Jill said, handing Josie the black puppy.

"I think he's excited to meet his new family," Josie said.

"How can you tell?" I said, glancing over.

"He just peed on me," Josie said.

"Occupational hazard," I said, laughing.

"Yeah, the life of an elf is never easy."

We completed the short drive and made our way up the steps to the Williamson's front door. Josie stood behind me holding the puppy that was wrapped in one of the Christmas doggy blankets we had bought just for this. I knocked on the door and was greeted by a young girl around five. Her parents stood behind her with huge smiles on their faces.

"Santa!" she exclaimed when she saw me standing at the door.

"Ho-ho-ho! Merry Christmas, Melissa."

"You're early," she said as she stared up at me.

"I am?" I glanced at her parents who laughed and shrugged their shoulders. "Well, I guess I am a bit early, but since you've been such a good girl this year, I decided there was no reason to make you wait any longer."

"I have been good, haven't I?" she said.

"Well, that's what my elves tell me," I said. "Now tell me again, my memory isn't what it used to be. What was it you wanted for Christmas?"

"A puppy," she said, looking up at me with a wide-eyed stare.

"Ho-ho-ho! That's right. You wanted a puppy," I said, moving to one side to reveal Josie holding the puppy. "Merry Christmas, Melissa. His name is Wilber."

The little girl hopped up and down several times, then reached out her arms. Josie gently placed the dog in her arms, and she squealed with delight.

"Thank you, Santa. Thank you, thank you, thank you. You too, Mr. Elf."

"You're very welcome, Melissa," I said. "You make sure you take good care of him."

"Oh, I will, Santa. I promise," she said, turning around to look at her parents. "Can I go play with Wilber in the living room?"

"Sure, honey," her mother said.

Melissa removed the blanket and put the puppy on the floor. Then they disappeared from view.

"Thanks, guys," the mother said. "That was perfect."

"You're welcome. She's going to do great," I said.

"He's doing pretty well with the housebreaking," Josie said. "But you should probably get him outside every couple of hours for the next week at least. For the moment, he's in good shape."

Josie spread her arms and showed them the large wet spot on the front of her elf costume.

"Oh, no. I'm so sorry," she said, chuckling.

"It happens all the time," Josie said.

"Can we get you anything?" she said.

"No, we need to get going. Merry Christmas, Linda. You too, Jimmy."

"We'll see you guys soon," Josie said. "Thanks so much."

"Yeah, thanks so much. Well done," the father said. "Have a great Christmas."

We waved goodbye and slowly made our way back to the SUV. We climbed in, and Josie checked our delivery list.

"Mr. Elf?" I said, laughing. "That's a first."

"It's gotta be the hat," she said.

Over the next hour and a half we delivered puppies to some very happy kids, and when we were down to our final puppy, Jill handed him to Josie already wrapped in one of the blankets.

"You can just let me out here," Jill said.

"Thanks again, Jill," Josie said.

"No, thank you. It was fun," she said, climbing out of the car. "I'll see you guys soon."

We drove off and turned right at the next stop sign. Two more right turns later, I pulled into a parking spot and turned the car off. Josie and I walked up the sidewalk, climbed the short set of steps and I knocked on the door. Josie took her position behind me, and we waited for the door to open.

"Well, what do we have here? Hello, Santa. What a nice surprise."

"Hi, Sammy," I said. "Merry Christmas."

"What? I don't get a ho-ho-ho?" he said, laughing. "Jill said the puppy deliveries were a lot of fun."

"Yeah, they were great," I said.

"Say, where's Josie?" Sammy said.

"That's odd," I said, "She was just here a minute ago."

Then I took a couple of steps to my left.

"Merry Christmas, Sammy," Josie said, holding Tripod out to him.

"Really?" he said, stunned. "You're giving him to me?"

"Who else?" Josie said.

185

Jill came up behind Sammy and put an arm around his shoulder.

"I suppose you knew all about this," Sammy said, not even bothering to try stopping the tears that were rolling down his cheek.

"Of course," Jill said. "Merry Christmas, sweetheart."

She gave him a kiss and Sammy gently accepted Tripod from Josie.

"Hey, bud," Sammy said, rubbing the puppy's head. "How you doing, Tripod?"

"We only have one condition," I said.

"What's that?" Sammy said.

"You have to agree to bring him to work with you," Josie said.

"That won't be a problem," he said, beaming at us. "You guys want to come in?"

"No, we need to get home," I said. "This beard is incredibly itchy."

"And my feet are killing me," Josie said. "Plus, we have to take care of a few things."

"Of course. I understand completely," Sammy said, laughing. "What's Chef Claire making?"

"Gumbo."

"Sounds great. Well, enjoy. You've certainly earned it," Jill said.

"What can I say? Bringing joy to young children always makes me hungry."

Epilogue

Christmas morning was quiet around the house as Josie and Chef Claire, along with Chloe and me, opened presents. Santa was good to all of us, and our gifts to each other ran the gamut from the practical to the thoughtful to the downright silly.

Captain was too young to open his new chew toys by himself, but I knew that by this time next year, he'd be strong enough to open whatever presents he chose to sink his teeth into. The Newfie was getting bigger by the day and a constant companion of Chloe who loved having the puppy by her side.

Around noon my mother stopped by to exchange gifts. As always, she went overboard and got me way too much stuff. When I began my annual protest about her extravagance, she reminded me that it was her money, I was her daughter, and my choices were to either enjoy the presents she bought for me while she was still around, or get a slightly bigger inheritance after she was gone. Unable to imagine my world without her in it, I shut up and opened the next present.

My mother can stop a conversation faster than Josie goes through a Snickers.

She stayed for lunch, then headed off to meet her new boyfriend at an undisclosed location. Normally, my mother was very open about the men she was dating, but she was playing this one very close to the vest. That meant that she either considered her new beau a potential keeper and didn't want to do anything that might potentially jinx the relationship, or he was more of the catch and release variety she didn't want anyone to know about.

I wasn't worried. I'd figure out a way to get it out of her eventually.

Since we'd given Sammy and Jill a couple of days off to enjoy the holidays, we were on duty. We'd also been keeping a close eye on the pregnant German shepherd and around four, when we were down at the Inn to feed the dogs and let them out to exercise, the shepherd started to go into labor. So we both changed into our scrubs and began a ten-hour watch that culminated in the successful delivery of a litter of six puppies and a very tired mama dog.

Around seven, just after the first puppy was delivered, Chef Claire stopped by the Inn with our dinner. We left the condo and headed to my office. As Chef Claire was passing around bowls of gumbo and sandwiches, I noticed the shiny object loosely wrapped around her wrist.

"Wow," I said. "That is a gorgeous tennis bracelet, Chef Claire."

She held her arm up and gently shook it and the bracelet sparkled in the light.

"It's beautiful, isn't it?" she said, sitting down to eat.

"Who's that from?" Josie said.

"I think it's from Freddie," Chef Claire said.

Confused, I glanced at Josie who also seemed clueless.

"You think?" I said. "You don't know who gave it you?"

Chef Claire put her sandwich down and then held up her other arm that displayed an identical tennis bracelet.

"No way," Josie said, laughing.

"Yeah," Chef Claire said.

"Freddie and Jackson got you the same thing?" I said, staring at the bracelets.

"Identical," Chef Claire said. "Right down to the wrapping. For a moment, I thought I was having a deja vu moment."

Josie and I roared with laughter.

"Well, I guess it's nice to know they both have similar tastes," Josie said.

"What is a girl to do?" I said, unable to stop laughing.

"Shut up," Chef Claire said, picking up her sandwich. "I was in the kitchen and heard a knock on the door. It was Freddie. We exchanged gifts, he stayed for about an hour, and we made plans to have dinner next week, then he left. Fifteen minutes later, Jackson showed up, and I swear we had the exact same conversation. It was like they had planned it. They wouldn't do that would they?"

"I seriously doubt it, Chef Claire," Josie said. "I don't think either one of them is in the mood to share their strategies with each other when it comes to you."

"Yeah, you're probably right," Chef Claire said. "But it was really weird."

"So what are you going to do?" I said.

"I don't know," she said. "Maybe wear them both. Or neither one."

"Just wear one," Josie said. "That will keep them guessing about which one of them might be in your doghouse."

"You're terrible," Chef Claire said, laughing.

"I think the word you're looking for is evil," I said.

"Hey, we're about to enter the winter doldrums, and we'll need something to help get us through it," Josie said.

"Yeah, you're right," I said, chuckling. "Wear one."

Chef Claire headed back up to the house, and we returned to the shepherd's condo where the second puppy was on its way. I sat down and stroked the mother's head as she continued through the deliveries, while Josie checked the status of each puppy. When the last puppy arrived, we helped the mother clean the puppies and made sure they were all warm and comfortable. Josie sat with her back against the side of the condo and stretched her legs out.

"I'll take the first shift," Josie said, yawning.

"Okay. I'm going to grab a shower, and I'll be back in a couple hours," I said.

"Perfect," she said. "Just wake me up if I doze off."

I started to head for the rear entrance that led up to the house then stopped.

"Oh, I almost forgot," I said. "I got you one more present."

"Suzy," she said. "You didn't have to do that. You always go way overboard."

"I saw this one and thought of you immediately."

"You're too much," Josie said, shaking her head.

I reached into my pocket, removed a bag of bite-sized Snickers, and tossed it to her.

"Oooh, how did you know?" she said, snatching the bag out of the air. "It's exactly what I wanted."

"Yeah, I know," I said. "Merry Christmas."

"Merry Christmas, Suzy."

I started up the path to the house pulled forward by the smell of gingerbread as I heard the sound of Christmas carols being sung somewhere off in the distance accented by the soft, mouse-like crinkling of tiny presents being unwrapped.

48545683R00111

Made in the USA
San Bernardino, CA
29 April 2017